# BLUE IGUANA

# blue iguana

### WENDY TOWNSEND

namelos
South Hampton, New Hampshire

Library of Congress Control Number: 2013931018

ISBN 978-1-60898-157-1 (hardcover : alk. paper)
ISBN 978-1-60898-158-8 (paberback : alk. paper)
ISBN 978-1-60898-159-5 (ebook)

www.namelos.com

*For Jessica, Eldemire, Sara, Yellow,*
*Matthias, Pedro, and Digger*
*And for young field biologists everywhere*

*Cruelty is surely the very worst of human sins.*
—Jane Goodall


*In the greens and earth tones of Grand Cayman's dry shrublands, the bright blue of* Cyclura lewisi *shines out like a beacon.*
—Fred Burton

# prologue

I remember when I was little and went with my dad to collect eggs at the Bryer Farm. What happened behind the chicken coop plays in my head like a silent movie. The snake goes up in the air, carried on the blade of a shovel, whole and alive, his scales glistening blue-black in the sun. Then he lands on the grass with a bounce. My heart speeds up when the blade comes down and I try to yell, but instead I vomit and drop the basket of eggs. I see the shovel come down again and again. His coils flip and roll on the bloody grass, and he is folded back on himself trying to bite the pain. My eyes are full of tears, and I run with fists and grab the shovel and try to pull it away. Things get blurry. Again I see the blade come down, this time chopping off his head, almost. The writhing slows. The snake's mouth is open and no sound comes out. I run and my dad calls, "Clarice!" but I keep running and praying, *He has to be dead, he has to be dead.*

part one

On Saturdays I volunteer at the SPCA a few miles up the road. When the weather's nice I ride my bike. One morning there's a cage by the door, with a cat inside, paws tucked under his chest. He's gray with long fur, like the kitten I had once. I squat beside the cage and see that he's got the same yellow eyes and tufts of fur on his ears.

When the supervisor gets off the phone I ask, "What's up with the cat?"

"Another night drop. Pretty, isn't he? Part Angora, or Persian, maybe. Someone will take him if he's nice. I haven't had a minute to find out." She tosses me a package of cat treats from the box on the counter and says, "Good luck," just as the door opens and a black Lab on a leash bursts through, pulling a kid out of breath.

I take the cage back to the office and shut the door. Beside the desk there's an old rug, and I sit down cross-legged. "Kitty," I say. Our eyes meet, and he doesn't seem afraid. I open the cage. The door swings to the side, and I keep it back with my knee. "Are you hungry?"

I tear open the packet and let some of the meat-smelling treats fall into my hand. His brick-colored nose works, and his eyes are round, watching, ears and whiskers forward. I hold the food out to show him and then put it down, leaving my hand there. When he comes to eat I scratch his cheek with my finger, and soon he is pressing the top of his head into my palm, eyes squeezed shut, purring loud. Slow and easy, I rub the soft fur around his neck and he keeps purring. But when I raise my hand to pet his back, he spits and shrinks into the corner, and my heart thumps from the sudden change. He

1

growls when I move, and his eyes are a half-moon shape, glaring. He's been hit or kicked, and won't ever be adopted.

Sometimes when I'm angry about someone hurting an animal on purpose I imagine that I have a sword, a long, sharp one, and I draw it with a *shing!* But nothing happens; the image fades, and I'm left feeling like there's nothing I can do. I shut the cage door. It's not fair. He shouldn't have to die just because somebody abused him.

I leave the cat in the office and go up front. "He's totally schizophrenic."

"Too bad."

"I'm taking him."

"Clarice," the supervisor says, shaking her head. She sighs. "We'll do the FLV test and his shots, then."


The next Saturday Dad picks me up from the shelter with the cat. I cover the cage with a sweatshirt and put it behind the cab of the truck and strap it in with a bungee cord while Dad loads the bike.

I've already had the talk with my parents. Dad said, "The fifth cat, Clarice."

Mom said, "What about when you go to college?"

"Joe will feed them," I said. Joe's my little brother. Really, my parents are more concerned about my college plans than they are about how many cats are living in the barn.

Dad backs the truck up to the barn door and I carry the cage inside and set it down by the food bowls. When I pull away the sweatshirt, the cat spits and growls. I open the cage door and walk back toward the house.

Joe is in the sandbox talking to Rod, his pet millipede. Whatever he's saying, it's more than he says to people. He's autistic. I step into the sandbox and sit down. There are no yellow dump trucks, no blue plastic buckets with red shovels. Instead there are small huts made of tree bark with patted-down paths connecting them. They are for Rod and for Joe's other friends, who are earthworms, beetles, caterpillars, and newts.

"We have a new cat," I say. "He wants to be petted, but he's afraid."

Joe's hair is getting long and the bangs hide his eyes when he's looking down, which is most of the time. He pats the sand, smoothing the path for Rod, who is slowly going in a straight line. Rod can go fast, I've seen him. But I've never seen him coil up, which is what millipedes do when they're threatened. There's a photo of one doing that in the field guide to spiders and insects.

I pull my knees to my chin. "Nobody's ever going to hurt this cat again."

Joe puts his hand by the path and Rod climbs in as if wanting to be there. When I watch my brother with one of his bug friends, everything slows down. The screen door slaps and I see Mom wave from the porch.

"Dinner," I tell Joe. We go inside and take Rod upstairs to the terrarium, and then we sit down at the table. It's roast chicken for them and tofurkey for me. I don't eat or wear animal products.

Mom says, "Did you get your cat settled in?"

"Sort of. He's a little angry right now. Traumatized from riding in the truck."

"What's his name?"

"Tufty. He's got these tufts of fur on his ears." I'm not clever with names. The cats have predictable ones like Patches for the calico and Redford for the orange tabby.

Mom smiles. "You'd make a wonderful veterinarian."

"Yeah, but you need straight A's in science. I'd never get into vet school."

Dad says, "You will if you want to bad enough."

Later I go up to my room and sit at my desk. Mr. Bloom is giving a bio test and I should study. I don't see how it will help, though. Last fall I studied hard for the cell bio test. I loved looking at electron micrographs of cells to see how organelles function. But I barely passed. Before the genetics one I stayed up way too late reading about animal behavior and evolution when I was supposed to be going over amino-acid sequencing. I still got a C on that one, just because I've gotten pretty good at figuring out multiple-choice tests.

I open my journal, or maybe I should call it a sketch-book—there are no lines on the pages, and it's filled with drawings of animals and little notes about what I see them do. I draw Tufty, his eyes wild and shaped like half-moons. I write, *How could anyone hurt a cat?* and even though it's corny I make little hearts around him.

My school notebooks are covered with flowering vines

and little frogs, so everyone knows I can draw, which is why they elected me to do the set for *A Midsummer Night's Dream*. I'm painting a forest on this huge canvas backdrop and it's got all these bugs and flowers that are larger than life. I was afraid I couldn't finish on time, until Polly started helping. She's a senior and she's playing Hermia. We just started talking one day when she was on break from rehearsal and came over to see how the set was coming. Turns out she doesn't eat meat either. Before, I ate lunch alone, because I couldn't stand the sight and smell of meat on other kids' trays. But now, Polly and I go to the auditorium and sit on the stage and eat our veggie sandwiches out of paper bags and look at the painting.

"I love the giant purple butterflies," she says. "Plus the way the trees are, with the trunks so thick and going all the way up? It's like you're really in the forest."

"The ants are the best," I say. It was Polly's idea to put them in, shiny black with waving antennae, marching over the blades of grass and big leaves. I uncross my legs and lean back on my hands. "Mr. Bloom would point out that we've got plants and animals that wouldn't exist in the same habitat."

Polly and I have been friends only three weeks, but I told her my big secret about the crush I had on Mr. Bloom for the whole of tenth grade. She waves her hand in the air. "Methinks you should pay him no mind. He doth lack imagination."

. . .

5

On Friday, I get the bio test back with a C– in red ink. Even though I'm over Mr. Bloom, the crappy grade stings. But that afternoon Polly and I finish the painting, and to celebrate we climb into her old Chevy and go into town for pizza.

We get a table by the window and order a large pie with peppers and mushrooms. I pick the cheese off my slice while Polly talks about New York. She's already been there to look for an apartment. "I'm taking a year off before college," she says. "And I'm going to be an actress."

"You already are." I love how Polly talks about what she's going to do.

Lifting her can of Sprite in both hands, she says, "I'd like to thank the Oscar committee." Then, "I bet you go to art school." Her eyes get big. "Cooper Union! It's in the village—we can go to coffee shops and sit by the window, like now, and watch people go by. It's the coolest thing—"

A crack of thunder makes me jump, and the flash of lightning stops time for a second. "That was close."

We hurry to the car as it starts to rain, and Polly fishes in her pocket for the keys. A horn honks, and then a pickup goes by with a couple of guys shouting, "Babes!"

Polly waves back, yelling, "Woo-hoo!" and she gets in the car with her cheeks all flushed and the rain in her hair.

"You're totally wild."

"They were cute," she says, starting the engine. I fasten my seat belt. Fat raindrops splat on the windshield as we go up Main Street to the end of town. "That'll be another cool thing about the city. Guys. The trouble here is, it's such a small school."

"Tell me about it."

"Poor Clarice. Wait till you go to college."

"That's what everyone keeps saying."

Since it's Friday night, there's traffic even on the back road. The wet asphalt glistens in the headlights and Polly turns up the wipers.

"Did you always know you wanted to be an actress?"

"Absolutely."

"*When* did you know? I mean, what made you—" I stop when a frog hops into view, making arcs in the headlights, and I hold my breath as he gets across.

"What were you asking?"

I can't answer, can't take my eyes off the road, because there are more frogs crossing. We pass over a big one, upside down, his leg kicking. I sit up fast. "He's still alive!"

"There's nowhere to pull over."

The leg kicking is inside my head now, and I think about being on the pavement, feeling the vibration of giant things roaring over me, the hot exhaust, blinding lights. A car comes up behind; the headlights force us to squint. Then we hit a frog, and I feel the awful *pop*.

Polly slows way down and leans forward, gripping the steering wheel with both hands. "There are so many." Cars go speeding around us. "There's nothing I can do."

"It's not your fault." I'm nauseous, but I keep watching the road until I see our mailbox. Polly makes a turn up the driveway and gets as close to the house as possible. I'm shaky unbuckling my seat belt.

"Don't take it so hard."

"I can't help it, I just—it's like I *feel* it, I'm in their bodies, feeling the pain."

"But what can you do?"

"I don't know." We sit there with the engine running and the rain beating down. The windshield wipers whip back and forth and I get a chill from the defroster blowing cold air. I say, "Polly, thanks. The set is awesome, and I couldn't have done it without you." Then I make a dash for the house.

"In here," Mom calls out. She's in the window seat with a book. I stand in the foyer.

"You're soaking wet. Is everything okay?" Mom finds a towel in the hall bathroom and puts it around me. "Did you have a nice time?"

"Yes, until I saw the massacre. The rain is bringing all the frogs out onto the road."

She rubs my shoulders, and I feel how tense I am.

"It's not like I haven't seen a few frogs on a rainy night. But this is bad." I shut my eyes and see their faces, mouths open. "Mom, why does it hurt so much?"

I let out a breath and look at the puddle my wet sneakers made. I go take them off by the door and follow my mom to the kitchen. She fixes us mint tea. She puts a spoonful of honey in each cup, and we sit down at the table. Breathing in the mint-smelling steam makes my stomach feel better.

"You ask why it hurts," Mom says. "I don't know what to tell you, except that you've always been sensitive. When you were three years old and tried to hold a salamander, his tail broke off and you cried so hard I'd have sworn it was you who lost the tail." She lifts the tea bag from her cup and sets it on the saucer. "But your sensitivity is a good thing. The way you are with Joe makes me wonder if you might like working with disabled children."

*Here we go again.* I stir my tea and watch the bag go round and round.

"You don't have to go far. There are perfectly good schools just a few hours from here."

"I'm not afraid to leave home. I just don't know what I want to *be*."

"When I was your age I didn't either. The whole point of college is to have time to sort it out. You'll gain confidence as you discover your capabilities."

"Great, except I can't think what they are, besides freaking out when I see roadkill." I don't sound nice. "Sorry, Mom."

"Honey, you just need to get out there and have new experiences, and college is the best place to start."

Joe appears in his red and blue Spider-Man pajamas. He opens his hand to show me Rod. Usually it's all he wants, to just show me his bug friends. But now Joe's trying to put Rod in my hand, so I flatten my palm and we all keep still while Rod makes his way from Joe's hand to mine. His many legs tickle my skin. When I read about millipedes in the field guide I found out that they don't actually have a thousand legs, but more like three or four hundred. I cup Rod in both hands and smile, showing Joe that I feel better now.

• • •

The next morning at breakfast Dad says, "How about you and me taking the truck out to the field for a driving lesson?"

When I got my learner's permit last summer, Dad tried to teach me. But the truck lurched and stalled every time I shifted into first—it's a standard—and I gave up. Now, Dad is looking at me all hopeful, so I say, "Okay."

In the middle of the field he stops the truck, gets out, and walks around to the passenger door. "Slide over, Clarice. You can't drive it from there."

We put on our seat belts again, and I step on the clutch and the brake and start the engine. Then I put my foot on the gas and let the clutch pedal up, and the truck jerks and stalls. I take my hands off the steering wheel and look at Dad.

"That's okay," he says. "It'll happen until you get the feel of it."

I start and jerk and stall. My hands get sweaty on the steering wheel. I try again and stall again. "I can't!" I say, dropping my hands in my lap.

"Be patient." He takes his clipboard out of the glove box and makes a drawing. "That's a standard transmission."

It looks like a mechanical mess, but as he explains what's happening when the clutch is released and how the gears mesh and the fuel reaches the engine, I start to understand.

"You ready to try again?"

"Okay." I step on the clutch, turn the key, and push the stick into first while releasing the clutch pedal and easing on the gas. The truck jerks, but then it goes.

"I felt it," I say, steering and bumping over ruts in the field. "I got it! Now what?"

"Put it in second."

I do and the truck goes faster, and I'm giddy with success. Dad tells me to stop the truck, restart it, and go through the gears again. It's rough, but I'm getting it, and then I'm actually driving up the dirt road that goes around the back of the field.

"Now drive into town," he says. "We'll get some of that frozen tofu stuff you call ice cream."

"Is that a good idea?"

"How else are you going to learn?"

I step on the gas and drive onto the road. The air blows on our faces and I relax my shoulders and ease my grip on the steering wheel. Polly will be so impressed. The road dips down through the swampy part and I hear spring peepers and think how nice it is to be going into town for ice cream with my dad. I see a frog and steer around him, but he hops and I yell, "No!" and swerve, and then I feel the *pop*. Breakfast is in my throat and Dad is saying, "Watch out! Ease up on the gas, step on the brake!" and he grabs the wheel and the truck goes onto the shoulder, stalls, and comes to a rough stop. I push open the door and let my breakfast drop on the asphalt. Then I wipe my mouth with the back of my hand and pull the door shut with a clunk.

Dad is quiet a moment. "Sweetheart," he says, "you can't do that."

"I know."

"Okay, but you *don't* know. Because if there had been another car, we would have been in trouble. Don't you see?"

"Yes. The frog is dead and I killed him. I was driving, and I killed him."

Dad lets out a long breath. "Jesus."


It's a warm sunny day, and Mom and I are peeling potatoes at the kitchen sink. Joe and the boys from up the road are playing in the sandbox.

I look out to see how it's going. Not so well. The two brothers are fine; it's the cousin who visits on weekends who's making things hard. He's twice Joe's size and seems too old to be playing with them. Now the kid is holding something just out of Joe's reach and I know it has to be some sort of bug—there's nothing else Joe would be trying so hard to take back.

"What do you think, Mom?"

"I think Joe's upset."

"I'll go," I say, wiping my hands on a towel.

When I get outside I see that the kid has Rod. The way he's holding him, his fingers are like big tweezers.

My heart speeds up and I walk quickly, without running, to keep things calm. "Whatcha got there?"

Before I can do anything, he pulls Rod apart. Joe cries out. I grab the kid by the arm. "You little shit."

He looks at me like, *What are you going to do about it?* I wrench his arm, digging in with my fingers, and I get my face in his. "How'd you like it if a giant came along and tore you in half and left you bleeding in the dirt?"

His face changes and he is about to cry, and I think,

*That's more like it.* The other two boys take off. The kid yelps. "You're hurting me!"

"Good." I squeeze harder and give him a shake before letting go of his arm. He rubs where I had a hold of it, and his eyes fill up.

"Go home," I say.

Joe is staring at the parts of Rod slowly twisting on the ground and he's tapping his leg, which he does when he's really upset. But the way he's staring makes a shiver go up my back, because his eyes are so vacant it's as though he's dying too. I want to take a rock and end it for Rod, but not with Joe here. So I bend down and gather the parts in my hands and put them in one of the tree-bark huts. Later, we can give Rod a proper burial. I take Joe's hand and we go inside.

Mom says, "You were pretty rough on that kid."

"That *kid* just killed Rod."

"Oh, no." She brings a hand to her forehead, and then she kneels beside Joe and tilts her head to see his eyes. "Darling? I'm so sorry."

Mom keeps still a moment, then holds his face in her hands. She kisses the top of his head before standing up. She and I look at each other. He's not crying, doesn't want to be hugged. It's as though he's just waiting for whatever comes next, and I'm relieved, because at least he's come back from wherever he went.

"Joe," I say. "Come help me feed the kitties."

As we walk to the barn I hold Joe's hand, which he lets me do, though he doesn't return my grip. I think about when it rains and a zillion earthworms drown in puddles and get run over by cars, and how Joe sees it—he sees everything. But every morning he gets up, brushes his teeth, and goes on with his day.

I lift the latch and open the door, and we step inside. Enough light comes in the small window to see that Redford and Patches have a vole that's still alive.

"Joe, don't watch."

He does, though. Standing perfectly still, he watches the cats play with the vole, whose back is broken. I don't see Tufty, but the two gray tabbies are crouched nearby, watching the poor creature drag himself toward a hay bale. Redford pounces and the vole squeaks.

My shoulders go up and I cover my eyes. "Haven't we seen enough, Joe?" I turn away. There's a garbage can full of cat food, kept shut with a bungee cord, and I take off the lid and scoop kibble into bowls. Then I dump the water bowl and refill it from a jug. I hear a scuffle of claws on wood and a small shriek and I want to run out of there, but I sit down on a hay bale. Joe's face is calm, lips together but not pressed. He knows what's going on; he's accepting it.

Patches picks up the dead vole in her mouth and carries it off behind the stacked hay. Redford follows. Joe comes to the food can and scoops out kibble until the levels are the same in both bowls. He puts the lid and cord back in place and looks at the water. I've done that right, so he leaves it alone.

Tufty squeezes through a space between two boards and freezes when I say, "Hi, kitty." He and Joe look at each other and his tail goes up and he rubs against Joe's leg and then goes to eat kibble. Patches and Redford appear, and soon all five cats are settled around the food bowls, crunching away, with Joe watching over them like Saint Francis.

.

In biology class Mr. Bloom tells us we are going to see something special. "This demonstration will enable you to understand a fascinating aspect of anatomy," he says, gesturing toward a small box with air holes punched in the top. "Now I'd like everyone to gather round so you can see."

Metal lab stools screech on linoleum and we find places to stand at the counter. Mr. Bloom takes out his dissection kit and opens it. I look at the shiny steel scissors and scalpels held in place on the red felt lining by elastic bands. The box moves and my pulse quickens. "What's in the box?"

Mr. Bloom raises a finger. "I'm glad you asked. We are going to observe atrial and ventricular systole and diastole in the frog heart."

He opens the box and takes out a frog. My heart starts racing.

"First, I'm going to pith the frog."

A student raises his hand. "What's 'pith'?"

Mr. Bloom lifts a dissecting needle from the kit. "I will insert a needle into the brain and sever the spinal cord, so that the frog will not feel pain when I cut it open."

"You can't do that," I say.

"The frog may crouch, try to jump, or even make noise, but it is not in pain."

"Don't believe it, people." By now the room is totally

quiet. "Just give me the frog and I'll let him go outside."

"This demonstration is an important part of your biology education."

"You've got to be kidding. It's called vivisection. Why can't you just *tell* us about the heart thing or draw it on the board?"

The frog struggles, and Mr. Bloom adjusts his grip until the legs go limp. "The others are here to learn. If you don't wish to participate, then take a seat."

I move, but not toward my seat. I go around the others to where Mr. Bloom stands holding the frog, whose throat pulses in and out. "Please give him to me," I say.

"Clarice, I'm going to dismiss you from class for today. I'd like you to go to Ms. Kling's office."

He stands there with the frog, his eyes on mine, and any lingering feeling of warmth I had for him vaporizes. Blood pounds in my ears and it's like I'm in a dream—a nightmare, because I want to take the scalpel and make him let go of the frog, but my feet are cement. Sweat runs down my sides. "I won't let you do this!" I hear my voice, almost a shriek.

"For Pete's sake, go to the counselor's office now or I'll have your parents called."

Again the frog struggles. Mr. Bloom is so angry that he's squeezing. My eyes fill and I run from the room.


In Ms. Kling's office I take another Kleenex from the box. "I said I wouldn't let him do it, but I did. I hope it's over now, I hope he's dead and out of misery."

Ms. Kling puts her hand on my arm while I'm trying to get my breath. "I'm so angry I don't know what to do. I never want to hurt anyone, but I wanted to hurt him."

I look at her and she doesn't flinch.

"I used to *like* Mr. Bloom. I'll never go back to that class, I don't care about failing." I wad up my sodden Kleenex. "What can be learned from torturing a frog?"

Ms. Kling's eyes search mine and I see her concern. It scares me. Her hand still rests on my arm. When my breathing steadies she sits back in her chair. After a moment she says, "What are your plans for the summer?"

I shrug and wipe my face. "Helping out with my little brother. Extra volunteer time at the shelter."

"I'm wondering if you might go and do volunteer work for wildlife conservation. Or you could assist with biology fieldwork, alongside graduate students."

"Me?"

"Of course. Why not? It will be good for you to meet people who are involved with animal welfare."

Ms. Kling sends me home with a note recommending that I take a day off from school.


I stay in bed the next morning and Mom comes to check my forehead. "You seem fine. How are you feeling?"

"I'm not sick."

"Ms. Kling says that you're pretty stressed and could use a change of scene." She picks up the pillow I kicked off in the night. "I like her suggestion about a summer program. Will you think about it and talk to your father or me?"

"Sure, Mom."

"Get some rest. I cut up that pineapple for you, and there's veggie soup in the fridge."

When the house is quiet, I go downstairs, still in my pajamas, and stand at the window. It's raining hard and the birds at the feeder can't relax. They shake their bodies and wings, but the rain is winning and the tiny feathers on their heads are streaked with wetness. I think about Mr. Bloom and I make fists and clench my teeth until my jaw hurts.

I'm supposed to be resting, so I go back to bed with a book and try to read. But the frog appears, his throat pulsing, and Mr. Bloom is pushing the pin into his head. I draw my sword with a *shing!*

That night I dream about a snake dying horribly, but somehow I help him. I wake up confused. There was no help for the snake. And none for the frog. At least it's over; he's not hurting anymore. I begin to let it go, which is troubling. Once Mr. Bloom told us that when a stimulus is repeated, the brain adjusts and the response gets weaker. I throw back the covers and get up and pull on jeans and a sweatshirt. My rage response toward him will never weaken.

At breakfast Joe opens his hand to show me a new friend. I slip my hand under Joe's and admire the little creature. He has a lot of legs, but not as many as Rod.

"He's a roll-up bug," I say. "They roll up when they're scared." Obviously, this one isn't. "What's his name?" I ask.

Joe doesn't answer, but I know he'll tell us when he's ready to.

"How are you feeling, sweetheart?" Dad asks me.

"Pretty good, I guess."

"Okay," he says, filling his travel mug with coffee. "We'll talk more tonight." He and Mom kiss, and he leaves for work.

"There's tomato soup, and some of that nice corn bread," Mom tells me.

Joe takes his Spider-Man lunchbox and stops. We look at each other. "I'm okay, Joe, really. Have a good day at school."

He goes to put on his jacket in the entry. Mom kisses my cheek and follows him out the door.

In the living room, I find the field guide to invertebrates. It says the roll-up bug is a wood louse, and that he's actually a crustacean, related to crabs and lobsters, which I find totally fascinating.

I take the package of vegan oatmeal cookies and a glass of soy milk up to my room and turn on the computer. After typing in "conservation volunteer" I hit the return key and look at the list. I click on the first one, "Sea Turtle Conservation in Costa Rica." There's a photo of hands cupping a baby turtle, and a list of responsibilities: *Dig up nests and transfer eggs to hatchery, protect eggs from predators, collect data about breeding and nesting.* I'm not too sure about the data part and go back to the main page. Near the bottom I see "Critical Assistance Needed, Blue Iguana Recovery Program." I click on it and a huge lizard appears, blue all over his head and shoulders. The whites of his eyes are red. His name is Yellow. I read about the yellow beads in his crest that are a tag for the research team. I scroll down and there's a photo of two people in khaki pants and hiking boots at the edge of a jungle, only instead of thick green foliage there are scraggly trees and rough-looking rock formations. The caption says, *Free at last! BIRP volunteers Meg and Josh emerge from a day in the Salina reserve, having released thirteen head-started iguanas in their new home.*

Under "Program Goals" I read about how the Grand Cayman blue iguana is found nowhere else on earth and that he is "functionally extinct." Farther down it says they need volunteers to feed baby iguanas, assist with fieldwork, and do landscaping in the pens. There's a photo of sweaty people with shovels. Some of them look about my age. Out the window, a movement catches my eye—a blue jay landing on the edge of Joe's sandbox. Joe knocked down the huts and all that's left is Rod's burial mound. I think about what happened to Rod, and Joe's face when he saw it, and I wonder if I should be going anywhere.

I go back to the blue lizard named Yellow. He peers into the camera lens, and for some reason my throat tightens. The only lizards I've seen are little green chameleons at the pet shop. Again I scroll down to the photo of the two volunteers. Meg and Josh. There's something about the way they're standing there, tired but happy. I bookmark the link and throw the empty cookie package in the trash. Pink flamingoes fill the computer screen, wings flapping, long necks stretched out. They fade into a mass of monarch butterflies. Next will be a coral reef, with a school of shimmering fish, but I'm already on my way down the stairs, heading for the barn.

Cats with their tails up weave around my legs while I fill bowls with kibble and change water. My mind is all over the place. Tufty rubs against me, but I don't try to pet him. I'll have to get a passport. And the plane ticket—I hope it's not too much. While the cats eat, I sit on a hay bale and try to see myself working at BIRP. Feeding baby iguanas sounds more like fun than work. So does releasing them back into that reserve. But I can't get a clear picture of assisting with fieldwork.

One by one the cats leave the food bowls to find places in the barn for a nap. Outside the sky is clearing, and sunlight comes through the dusty window and falls on my hands. I notice how pale they are, almost ghostly, as if I'm not all here. The stillness hits me and I get an ache that feels desperate, but not in a bad way, and for what, I don't know. I rub my hands together even though they are not cold. Maybe I need to go and find out about these big blue lizards and see if I can help them—maybe see what makes those two volunteers look happy.

At dinner I put broccoli and a salmon steak on Joe's plate and a slice of vegan lasagna on mine. I unfold my napkin and rearrange the silverware, placing the fork, spoon, and knife so they are perfectly aligned beside my plate. Mom brings the salad and Dad follows with a bottle of wine. He pours some in Mom's glass, then his, before sitting down. "Everybody have a good day?"

Joe picks up a broccoli stem. I get my right foot to stop jiggling my leg up and down.

Mom says, "Clarice, what's going on?"

"I found something on the Internet." I tuck my hair behind my ears. "Helping to save a species of lizard from going extinct."

"Okay," Dad says. "We'll have a look after dinner."


Dad sits at the computer in his office, Mom pulls up a chair, and Joe stands between them, watching the screen. I grip the back of Dad's chair. "*B-I-R-P*," I tell him, and he types it in.

"Wow," he says.

"That's Yellow."

"He looks blue to me."

"He's called Yellow because of the beads. For the research team?"

Dad clicks on "Program Goals" and sees the photos of volunteers. "They look like my crew after a ten-hour day."

"So it's in the Caribbean," Mom says. "Go to 'Accommodations.'"

Four small cinderblock buildings sit in a clearing surrounded by exotic-looking trees. It says the showers and kitchen are communal.

"Not so different from a college dorm," Mom says.

"It doesn't cost anything, I just have to get there. And I guess some money for food."

"That won't be much," Dad says, teasing me.

I nudge him.

Mom says, "Click on 'What to Bring' and print it."

. . .

Ms. Kling talks to Mr. Bloom about whether he'll accept an essay from me on dissection and ethics. He agrees that if I do a good job he will give me a C– instead of a D for my final grade. So for the last two weeks of school I go to study hall instead of bio class and work on the paper. It's hard at first—I'm so angry about what he did to the frog that I can't even write an outline. But then I realize it's my chance to make my case about cruelty to animals. I write down all the points of my argument, and I back them up with excerpts from my favorite book by Temple Grandin.

On graduation day, when Polly goes on stage to accept her diploma, I clap and yell, "Woo-hoo!" as loud as I can. Afterward, people stand around in little groups, the graduates in their caps and gowns, family in dresses and nice pants. I give Polly a long hug and promise to send a postcard.

"Have an awesome trip," she says.

"Yeah. I will," I say, standing on my tiptoes. "I'm still kind of scared."

"But it's the coolest thing! You're going to save the blue iguanas."


A week later it's Saturday morning, and I'm looking around my room one last time—we're leaving in five minutes. It hits me that I want something of Joe's to take along. I go to his room and get a book off the shelf. *Peter Pan.* I used to read it to him. His favorite was the crocodile with the clock inside. Softly, I'd go, "Tick-tock, tick-tock," and he would get very still, watching my face, watching my mouth make the words. I put the book in my backpack and carry my bag downstairs and walk out to the car, where Joe is waiting patiently in the back seat.

Mom and Dad follow with their travel mugs of coffee, and when we're all in with our seat belts on, Mom says, "Ready?" She starts the car and we go down the driveway.

Joe is wearing his blue and gray Batman shirt. "It's only for the summer," I tell him. "I'll be home before you know it."

He opens his hand to show me the wood louse. "Poley," he says.

"'Poley'? How'd you come up with that?" I take Joe's other hand. His fingers curl and uncurl in mine. "I'll write," I say. "Maybe send you some cool postcards. And don't forget, you're in charge of the kitties now."

"Did you get those things from behind the seat?" Mom asks.

"Yes," I say, reaching for the shopping bag. Everything goes in my backpack—sunglasses, barrettes, sunscreen (the kind with the "Not tested on animals" sticker), the packets of powdered soy milk, and the vegan energy bars.

"Stamps and envelopes?"

"Uh-huh."

Mom catches my eye in the mirror. "I'm envious. What an adventure."

"Well, you've been all over Europe."

"Sure, but I was a tourist."

I squeeze Joe's hand. At the airport Mom pulls over at the DEPARTURES sign. "I'll stay with the car," Dad says. He takes my bag out and sets it down at my feet. It isn't heavy, no coat, no sweaters. I hug him. "Work hard," he says. "But try to have some fun."

As we go inside the terminal I think Joe may be getting that something's up. He's got my hand in a tight grip, which is odd. We check in and find the security area, where only passengers can go. I see my gate on the other side.

"Got something to read?" Mom asks.

"The Cayman Islands guidebook."

"Cash? Think you have enough?"

"Yes, and if not, I have the card. Don't worry, Mom, okay?"

They announce the flight to Miami, where I'll change planes. We hug and then I tell Joe, "I need my hand back." I bend down and put my arms around him, and he goes limp. "Bye-bye, Joe," I say.

He looks at me with his calm brown eyes. Mom takes his free hand and leans in to give me one more kiss. "Bye, sweetie."

She turns and they walk toward the exit. I watch to see if Joe looks back, but he doesn't, he just trots along at Mom's side, one hand in hers, his roll-up bug in the other.

part two

The plane starts to move and I tighten my seat belt. Out the window I see pavement, wide runways that go on and on, with patches of weeds in between. Another plane lands as we're picking up speed. Metal thunks in the belly; then we're off the ground and I get a rush, feeling this massive machine pulling me forward impossibly fast.

I watch the houses and trees getting smaller as we climb, and soon the cars are slow-moving dots on a grid of lines. Puffs of clouds like shredded cotton are moving into view. The plane dips, then pulls up, making my insides weightless. Suddenly we're above the cloud blanket, and all I can see is blue sky.

When the flight attendant brings lunch I see that everything has animal products, so I say no thanks and get an energy bar out of my backpack. I start flipping through a magazine filled with ads for where to eat seafood, play golf, go scuba diving. There's a map of the West Indies and I find Grand Cayman. The island looks sort of like a sperm whale with his tail up as if he is playing. I touch the place that would be his eye, where the Queen Elizabeth II Botanic Park is. And BIRP. I focus on finding Georgetown, and the airport.

The first thing I do in Miami is look at the monitor for the flight to Grand Cayman. It doesn't leave for a couple of hours, so I walk through the terminal. All these flights are coming and going from around the world, especially South America. Whenever they make an announcement they do it in Spanish as well as English. I go into a gift shop and see little alligators, real ones, varnished, with glass eyes. Some are about to swing a miniature tennis racket, and some hold fishing poles. All of them wear Barbie doll-sized T-shirts that say WELCOME TO FLORIDA. I glare at the sales clerk even though she didn't kill them, and I get out of there, gripping my backpack strap. I bump into someone pulling a suitcase on wheels and say, "Sorry." I stand still while people hurry around me with baggage and babies in strollers. Reading the overhead sign with gate numbers and arrows, I see that I'm going the wrong way. I turn back and sit down at my gate and look through the Cayman Islands guidebook while I wait for the plane to board.

When we fly over the ocean it's so deep blue it's almost black. The water shimmers with reflected sunlight and there are flecks of white, the crests of waves, but from so high up they don't seem to be moving. I wish Joe could see it. Soon there are cloud shadows and the blue is getting brighter, as if light is coming from under the water. I bet it's the white sand. In the distance are patches of brown—little cays—and the plane is flying lower. Then I see the big island. The shallow water looks like blue liquid glass, and there are dark brown patches beneath, maybe weeds or a coral reef. I wonder if I could see a shark from up here. As the plane flies lower I can see the water move, the white-capped waves rushing toward white sand beach, and then we're over land. I see a burst of yellow that looks like a giant bouquet of flowers rising above the scrub forest.

Approaching the runway we're still going so fast the landscape blurs. Then we're on the ground, and I feel the engine straining to slow the plane down. When the flight attendant opens the door, hot air floods the cabin. I drink the rest of the water in the bottle and put it in the trash bag on the way out. Squinting in bright sunshine I follow the other passengers down creaky aluminum steps and across the tarmac. The heat is dry, not humid the way it is back home. It hits me that I'm surrounded by miles of ocean. Then, in a crowd of people behind a fence, I see a girl in a T-shirt with a lizard on the front. It's Sandy—we emailed, and she told me she'd wear a BIRP shirt. I wave, our eyes meet, and she waves back and points to the doorway where passengers are lining up in front of booths. "I'll meet you on the other side," she calls out, and disappears inside the building.

I get in line under a big sign that says CUSTOMS AND IMMIGRATION. WELCOME TO GRAND CAYMAN ISLAND.


Sandy drives a Jeep that's all open. It's like we're in a Pepsi commercial, speeding down the road with palm trees on both sides and the wind in our hair. Sandy's got curly blond hair and a tan, plus she's wearing shorts and sandals. My jeans and sneakers are way too hot for the climate, and the heat is making me spacy. I can't seem to put together even one question.

"How was the flight?" Sandy asks.

"Seeing the ocean from way up was the best part."

"Oh, I know. You forget how big it is until you fly over it."

When we come to a stoplight Sandy takes off her sunglasses and wipes them with a bandana that's tied around the gear stick. Like me, she's not wearing any makeup or much jewelry, just little silver earrings like my kitty-face ones, except hers are shaped like lizards.

"What happens to the iguanas?" I ask. "Why are they so endangered?"

"Well, like anywhere, there's habitat loss. Then feral cats and dogs are a huge problem. Three weeks ago dogs got into the park and killed Sapphire."

I shudder. I've seen dogs kill a woodchuck.

The light changes, and Sandy shifts gears and steps on the gas. My nose feels like it's burning already, so I unzip my backpack and take out the sunscreen while we drive past hotels and expensive-looking shops. We go by a parking lot with rows of sheds that have thatch-palm roofs, and out in front are fruits and vegetables and people buying them.

"That's the market," Sandy says. "You can get everything. Coconuts, mangoes, beans, squash, fish."

Turning right at a big intersection, we go out of town on a road that's lined with a different kind of palm tree, not as tall, and with the upper part of the trunk smooth and green. We're driving on the left. I can't believe I didn't notice sooner. That's how out of touch I am as a non-driver. We pass a road sign with a lizard on it: iguanas have right-of-way. "Are they walking around out here?"

"Yeah, what few are left outside the park. They bask on the pavement sometimes and that's when they get hit."

"It's like that back home, with turtles and snakes. But there aren't any right-of-way signs."

"Where's home?"

"Pennsylvania."

"Yuck, as bad as Michigan. I hate the cold."

"So you've lived here a while."

"Three years and counting."

"Do you work at BIRP full-time?"

"Part-time. I'm majoring in tropical biology at the university. And I tend bar at the golf club."

"There's a university here?"

"Sure. GCIU."

"I'm supposed to be thinking about college."

"Jeez, I forgot you were still in high school. So what about college?"

"I'm still thinking."

"Got a boyfriend?"

"No. You?"

"I met a guy when I came down here. We split up on New Year's Eve."

"That's sad. How come?"

"He wanted someone more . . . more 'ambitious'— that was the word he used."

"Sounds like kind of a jerk."

"He wasn't entirely wrong." She puts on the signal and goes off the paved road onto one that's white gravel. "I mean, I don't have any big career plans, at least not now. I just like working with the iguanas. Wait till you see them. Did you ever meet a lizard who looks you right in the eye?"

"No, but that photo of Yellow on the BIRP site is intense."

White dust from the gravel is getting kicked up,

though we're not going fast at all. It smells like salt and stone. On both sides of the road are all these tropical plants I recognize from the garden section of Home Depot, only here they're big as trees. I keep looking ahead expectantly, as if a giant blue lizard will come out of the bush. "Can you pet them?" I ask.

"A few. Especially Digger, he's my darling. But most of the adults are pretty wild, and we try not to handle the head-start babies. They're hard to resist, though."

"Yeah," I say, "but it's better if they stay afraid of people."

Sandy takes a left and just ahead there's an iron gate that's open. On the bars metal silhouettes of two lizards face each other, like dragons guarding the entrance. We drive through and park next to a building that's basically a cinderblock box, with aluminum hurricane shutters. There's a sun-faded blue pickup with "BIRP" stenciled on the door. It's one of those Ford crew cabs like my dad used to have.

"The Mess," Sandy says. "It's where we eat and talk about what needs doing. Tom's office is inside, but he's in town for a meeting." She looks at her watch. "Jeez, you must be starving." She pulls my bag from the back seat.

"Not really." I shoulder my backpack and follow her up two steps onto a porch that looks out on a yard with no grass, just rough sand and white stones, and a little ways past is a low cement wall, like in a zoo. Sitting with their backs against the building are a guy and a girl in T-shirts and khaki trousers.

"Meg!" I say.

She laughs.

"Sorry. I recognize you from the photo. On the website?"

"Sure." She reaches up to shake my hand. "This is Josh."

"Hey, great to meet you," he says.

"How'd it go?" Sandy asks them.

"Everyone's fed and happy," Meg says.

"They *seem* happy," Josh says.

Meg knocks his elbow off his knee, playfully.

"These guys are usually out in the Salina until sundown," Sandy says.

Something makes me turn. A lizard, a cat-sized dinosaur, blue. He's got these muscular legs and walks with his belly off the ground and his long tail out behind. When I see the red eyes I gasp and my backpack slips off my shoulder, but I catch it before it drops. I hold still as the lizard jumps up on the porch and comes to rest in one fluid motion. He cocks his head to look at Sandy.

"Macho's got us trained to give him treats."

"Got *you* trained," Meg says.

There's a spiral cluster of miniature bananas tied to a hook in a porch post, and Sandy breaks one off. Macho takes it in one bite, peel and all. He reminds me of an alligator, the way he jerks his head back to gulp down food. Sandy tries to pet Macho, but he backs up. "He doesn't like being petted," she says.

"You don't know that he likes or doesn't like being petted," Josh says, "because he's never experienced it."

"Well, I know my Digger likes being petted." Sandy shields her eyes and looks out across the grounds. "Since it's getting late, the iguanas may be in their burrows, but I'll give you the nickel tour."

"We're heading over to Johnny's," Meg says. "Why don't you join us."

"What's Johnny's?"

"A little place up the road that makes the best grouper sandwiches on the island."

I learned from the travel guide that grouper is a fish, but I don't say anything about being vegan. Sandy breaks off more bananas and gives me a few. "To hold you till dinner."

I peel back the skin and take a bite. It's warm from being in the sun, and incredibly sweet. Just this morning I was home, having my breakfast shake with supermarket strawberries, and now I'm on a Caribbean island, eating a fresh-picked banana.

"The pens are laid out like a tic-tac-toe board," Sandy explains. "The big ones are for breeding pairs." We walk beside a wall that's about waist-high and I see little wooden signs with names painted on. Matthias and Arlington are in one pen, Billy and Deborah in another. Sandy points to a row of pens, each the size of my room back home. "Those are holding areas for singles. We've got Sara and Jessica in there until they recover from laying eggs. Then we have Eldemire—he's an old sweetie—and Pedro, and of course our poster boy, Yellow. And here," she says, climbing over, "is my boy, Digger."

I'm speechless, watching the blue lizard come running to Sandy.

"Yes, baby, Mama's got a treat." She gives Digger a banana, which he tears in half and eats in two bites. Then she scoops him up in her arms and kisses him on the neck. "He's my precious boy," she coos. The lizard holds on to her like a toddler, arms on her shoulders and legs around her ribs. "He'll put up with this for about two minutes."

A smaller lizard watches from across the pen. I can see the red eyes. "That's his mate?"

"Yeah, that's Elle. She's kind of shy." Sandy nuzzles the folds of skin at Digger's neck and his eyes get a sleepy, half-open look.

"He knows you."

"He knows I love him, too." She takes a step closer. "Feel how soft he is."

I put out my hand and touch Digger's shoulder. I've never touched a lizard before. He's warm and I can feel the muscle under his smooth, dry skin. And something else—his *aliv*eness. Of course, because he *is* alive, but something else, too, something that's not so easy to feel through the fur of a cat or dog.

He starts pushing against Sandy's shoulder.

"For heaven's sake," she says, bending to let Digger down. His tail slips through her hands and he goes to his mate, bobbing his head up and down fast, as if saying *Yes, yes, yes.*

"What's he doing?"

"Talking. No vocal cords, they bob heads instead. He's reminding her that he's in charge."

There's a flash of blue in the next pen. Another huge lizard has climbed up on a rock.

"Who's that?"

"Billy. He's too wild to pet."

I go over to see him. Sandy climbs out of Digger's pen. I look at Billy and he looks at me. I've still got a banana. "Can I give him this?"

"Sure."

I lean against the wall and hold out the fruit. Billy waits a second, then climbs down and comes close and looks up, right in my eyes, and I catch my breath.

"He won't take it from you."

I hold still another moment. Just as I'm about to drop the banana, he takes a step closer. He leans toward the fruit and reaches for it with his tongue, which is not like a snake's but fleshy and pink. I stretch out my arm, closing the gap, and he takes the fruit.

"Whoa," Sandy says. "Billy never does that. He is totally checking you out."

"What about teeth?"

"They're sharp, all right." She holds up her thumb, and I see a curved scar the length of it.

"Digger didn't mean to," she adds. "I was giving him meds, tucked in a plum, and I gave it a little push right when he was biting down."

"I bet that hurt."

"Oh, yeah." She turns her thumb to look at the scar. "I like it, though. It's my Digger mark."

"It is pretty cool."

Billy watches me, his belly resting on the ground, and I wonder what it would be like to hold him.

"Sometimes you get a hot shower, sometimes you don't," Sandy tells me. We step inside a cinderblock building with no door. The windows are small, near the ceiling, and there's no glass. Below are two sinks and a mirror. It reminds me of a rest stop, only clean, and with shower stalls instead of toilets.

There are three more buildings at the edge of the forest. Between two of them stands a huge tree, shading part of both. The branches are like hands with gnarled fingers and the bark is green, with brown peeling skin, as if it's got sunburn. "It's a gumbo-limbo," Sandy says. "The birds love this tree and they'll be up with the sun, singing about it."

We go inside my room, which has a window facing the path that goes to the showers or back to the Mess. There's a desk at the window and a dresser painted white by someone in a hurry.

Sandy puts my bag down by the bed, which is a thick pad on a metal frame. Sheets and a blanket and pillow are stacked at one end. "Pretty stark," she says.

I set my backpack on the desk and look at the closet-sized bathroom.

"You won't be spending a lot of time here."

"I like it."

Sandy laughs.

"No, seriously, there's something about it," I assure her.

"Right, something uniquely monastic. So, are you hungry?"

"Yeah. Do I need to dress up?"

"Dress down. I'm wearing what I've got on. Get settled and meet me at the Mess when you're ready."

I pull off my sweaty airport clothes and put on shorts, a T-shirt, and sandals. I make the bed and then unpack, putting my clothes in the dresser, except for the khaki trousers, which go on a hook in the wall. My one dress goes on the same hook. Sneakers go beside the dresser, my toothbrush, towel, and pouch of earrings on top of it.

I splash water on my face and realize there's no mirror. If I want to see myself I'll have to go to the showers, so I skip it. I run my hands through my hair and check the backs of my kitty-face earrings to make sure they're still in place. Before pulling the door shut I take one more look at my room, with the bed made and my backpack on the desk.


Johnny's is another cinderblock box that looks like it dropped out of the sky and landed in a clearing. It's lit up with Christmas lights around the windows. I figure the food must be good, because there are maybe twenty cars parked. I smell fried food and hear the steady beat of reggae music.

Josh and Meg have a table and we join them. There's a blackboard menu on the wall decorated with palm trees and sailfish in blue and green chalk. The waiter asks, "Caybrew?" and Sandy says, "Sure, thanks."

I see caybrew on the beer in Meg's hand. "Apple juice?" I ask the waiter.

"Pineapple juice?" he says.

"Yes, please."

There's a gnarled scar on Meg's finger. Since I'm pretty sure I know what it is, I ask her for the details.

"That one I got from WGW," Meg says. "Better known as Wiggly Worm."

Sandy holds up her Digger mark. "You may have me beat."

Meg puts her finger next to Sandy's thumb. "Nah, they're the same."

The waiter comes back with drinks, and Sandy orders the grouper sandwich. I ask for a salad and basket of fries and wait for someone to say, "You don't like fish?"

Meg says, "We buy grass-fed meat from local farmers now. But Josh and I were vegan for a long time."

"Because you love animals, or for health?"

"For a healthy planet," Josh says. "Commercial meat production is bad for the environment."

"Not only that, it's cruel!"

Meg's eyebrows go up.

"Sorry. I get a little excited about it," I explain.

"What brought you here?" she asks.

"My counselor thought it would be good for me to get involved in conservation work. And my parents are worried about what I'm going to do with my life."

Sandy rolls her eyes. "Mine too."

"But you're in college. You have BIRP. You drive a car."

Meg says, "You don't?"

I shake my head. "When my dad was teaching me I hit a frog."

"Anyone who drives hits animals now and then," Meg says. "It's awful. But you know what? It's not your fault."

"It is if I'm driving the car."

"But you can't let that stop you from getting around."

"Well, where I live, animals get hit all the time. The worst part is when they don't die right away. It gives me nightmares." I pick up my glass and get a chunk of ice to chew on.

Josh says, "In England they've put tunnels under the roads in some places."

"You're kidding."

"Nope. They're called toad tunnels. They put a camera in one and let it run for twenty-four hours, then sped up the film to see the results. It was a wildlife superhighway—toads, newts, frogs, turtles, hedgehogs, mice, snakes."

"Why don't we do that here? I mean, in the States?"

"Money," Sandy says.

"Write to your representative," Josh says. "Get involved. That's how they did it in England."

I'm trying to imagine circulating a petition in my school when the waiter brings four baskets to the table— three with the fish sandwiches and fries, and one with salad in a red plastic bowl. Meg picks up her sandwich and bites into it. I watch her chew and swallow. Our eyes meet and she smiles. "Does it bother you when people eat meat?"

"No. Well, maybe a little. It used to really bother me.

I'd talk to kids at school during lunch. I'd tell them people weren't meant to eat animals. They'd look at me like I had antennae."

Josh says, "People don't like being told what they should or shouldn't eat."

"Yeah, I figured that out."

Meg says, "What about when animals eat animals?"

I hesitate. "It bothers me. I know it's silly."

Josh eats the last bite of his sandwich and wipes his mouth with a napkin. "There's a sect in India called the Jains. Heard of them?"

I shake my head.

"The Jains won't do any kind of work or activity that even remotely endangers animal life. Their core belief is non-injury to living things. They carry a small broom and sweep the ground before walking on it so they don't risk stepping on a bug. And they carry a cloth to hold over their mouths to protect against the ingestion of small insects."

I sit there looking at Josh. "That's totally admirable. How can they live like that?"

"Very, very carefully."

"I think my brother could be a Jain." I tell them about Joe.

"He sounds like a neat kid," Meg says. "He's your only sibling?"

"Yes, he was a surprise. My parents didn't plan on another after me, but then Joe happened. I can't imagine how life would be otherwise."

"Wow, that's so nice," Sandy says. "I'm an only child.

And the way things are going in my love life, I'll never have any."

"Gimme a break," Josh says. "You're a kid yourself, what's the rush?"

"I'm just whining." She puts down her beer and yawns. "I've got to get some rest. Tomorrow's a big day on the farm. Right, Clarice?"

"Uh-huh," I say, yawning too.

"It's catching," Josh says, and gets the check.

Sandy goes back to her apartment at GCIU. Watching the Jeep's taillights disappear I remember sitting in the back of Mom's Subaru just this morning, telling Joe I'd miss him. It seems like ages ago. I climb in the BIRP truck beside Meg and pull the door shut, and Josh drives out of the parking lot. Though he's driving slowly I get the same feeling I had on the plane, like I'm being pulled forward too fast. Warm wind blows through the cab and I rest my arm on the door, the way I do on a summer night when Dad and I go for ice cream.

Josh parks the truck and we walk to our rooms. "So," he says, "tomorrow you start."

"Excited?" Meg asks.

"I am. The iguanas are awesome."

A bat flies over our heads and we look up. No one says anything. Stars are out, but they're far away, not like the autumn sky when I could almost touch them. Josh breaks the silence. "Sleep well."

"You too."

I stand under the gumbo-limbo tree. The air is so warm

I'm comfortable in shorts, and there's a half moon rising. I think about what Josh said, about getting involved. When I was in second grade I wrote to the President. Our class had sent a letter about polar bears and drilling in Antarctica. Not only did the President write back, he sent someone in a suit and tie to give us a signed photograph and we got our picture in the *Times Record*. So I thought if I wrote to the President, someone would come visit me and I could talk about what happened to the black snake. Instead I got a letter that said, "Dear Mr. Taylor, thank you for your concern." The letter went on about how I could rest assured that everything was being done and so forth.

I reach inside the room, find the light switch, and push the doorstop in with my foot. After pulling the screen door shut, I look at my backpack on the desk. I'm too tired to write home. So I get into my extra-long T-shirt, turn off the light, and lie down on the bed. The pillow is kind of mushy and has a faint smell, like the dust from the white stone road.

Something chirps. At first I think it's a smoke-alarm battery going dead. *Chirp.* It's something alive. Another chirp, this time from the desk. I prop myself on my elbow and try to see in the dimness. On the wall are two dark spots that must be eyes with the pupils wide open. They move and I make out the shape of a small lizard. A gecko, the kind with the sticky toe pads. The one above me chirps and I see his eyes and lizard shape and I watch him waddle across the ceiling toward his friend. Coming here was a good plan. I start to drift and think of Billy, eating the banana from my hand, and the way he looked at me with his red eyes.

. . .

Birds wake me with their bright singing. I reach for the alarm clock and turn it off before it starts beeping. Sandy wasn't kidding: it sounds like a whole flock is up there on the roof. Light is filling the room and there's no sign of my gecko friends.

It's already hot, but a shiver goes through me: my first day on the job. I grab a towel and head for the showers. Halfway there I catch a glimpse of a crab big as my fist before he slips down a hole by the cinderblock wall. Joe would be able to coax the crab out.

The water's warm and it feels good to wash up after my trip. I dry off and put on sneakers, shorts, and a T-shirt and walk to the Mess. Sandy's Jeep is pulling in and right then a black cat runs from behind the building. Before he disappears in the bush I catch a glimpse of his fur, which is long, like Tufty's, but patchy and matted. Sandy comes up the steps at the far end of the porch.

"Morning," Sandy and I say at the same time. The smell of coffee wafts from inside and we follow it to the source.

"Oh, that's Meg," Sandy says, pouring us cups. "She knows how to make it strong."

The Mess kitchen has a sink and a stove, a long counter, and two humming refrigerators. Taped on one is a sign that says PINK; on the other, BLUE.

Sandy opens the pink one and gets out the milk. "Our refrigerators are color-coded. It's what you get when biologists try to be funny."

"Are Meg and Josh around?"

"No, by now they're deep in the Salina."

"The reserve?"

"Right, tracking head-start iguanas, gathering data. Sleep well?"

"I did, thanks."

"There's granola in the fridge. Help yourself."

I pour some in a bowl while Sandy goes out to cut bananas from the stalk. "There were two geckos in my room last night," I say through the window over the sink.

"They're all over the island," she says, bringing in a bunch of the little fruits.

I peel and slice three into my bowl. "I saw a cat this morning," I tell Sandy.

"Where?" she asks.

"Out behind the Mess."

"Tell Tom the next time you see it."

"What will he do?"

"Shoot it."

"But why? Can't we trap him?"

"And do what? The shelters are overcrowded and it'll just be euthanized."

"Okay, but why do we have to be so violent?"

"Stray cats eat lizards, Clarice. Including baby iguanas." Sandy looks at the clock on the wall. "We should get started on the feeding." She opens the blue refrigerator and takes out a cloth laundry sack. It's filled with all kinds of leaves, and flecks of yellow and pink that are flower petals.

"For the little ones we need to chop the leaves. Then

twice a week everyone gets some fruit, which has to be chopped and mixed in, or the quick ones get it all."

"How long do you head-start them?"

"Until they're too big for cats and birds. It takes a couple of years."

Sandy shows me how small to chop the salad, which goes into two five-gallon buckets. "When we're done with the babies, we'll come back and fill these with leaves for the big guys."

We carry the food and an inch-thick stack of paper plates out to the head-start iguanas. There are three rows of back-to-back cages. At one end is a post with a water spigot and a couple of empty buckets next to it.

"The bigger the lizards are, the fewer we have in each cage," Sandy tells me, turning on the spigot to fill buckets. "Feeding takes about four hours if you're doing it alone, which you will be when there's a tour group."

"To see the iguanas."

"Uh-huh."

When we get closer, dozens of baby lizards scramble up cage walls, their claws making a sound like a comb being scraped across a screen. Feeling bad that we're scaring them, I slow down.

Sandy goes right up to the cage. "These are last summer's hatchlings, and they're a little edgy around strangers."

One of the babies clings to the screen. As I walk around the cage his head turns and his eyes follow me. On his stomach I see the stripy pattern fade as the edges meet, and then I see a small line in the scales. "He has a belly button."

"Yes, an umbilical scar."

"God, that's cute."

"There's no end to cuteness around here." Sandy peels off a plate and loads it with salad. "You have to be careful when you open the cage, because if we lose a baby he could be taken by a hawk or a cat. Here's a little trick," she says, holding the plate up to the screen.

Right on cue, the babies climb down and run to it.

"Now you open the door and put the food inside. While they're digging in, you change the water." Sandy tips the bowl and the water falls through the screen. She fills it with fresh water from the bucket, then picks up the old paper plate, shuts the cage door, and latches it. "Easy. Just be alert. As you get to know them you'll see which ones are skittish."

We move to the next cage, and again many pairs of eyes watch me. Some of the babies are pressed against branches and rocks.

"They're trying to hide by making themselves smaller," Sandy explains.

I put salad on a plate and hold it up. "Look," I say, "breakfast." They just watch me.

"Go ahead. They're fixed on you, because you're unfamiliar."

They don't budge while I unhook the latch, open the door, and put down the food. Some watch my hand; some keep their eyes fixed on mine. I have the impulse to touch one, but I move quickly to get the job done. The moment I finish, the babies rush in to eat, as if they feel safer when the door is shut.

"Perfect," Sandy says, and we move to the next cage, which goes smoothly as well.

After that, Sandy picks up the other food and water buckets. "I'll go to the ones on the end and work my way back. We'll meet somewhere in the middle."

I do five more cages with little babies, and then I'm into the row with the two-year-olds. They are alert but not so frightened, and they totally fall for the food trick. Except for one, in the cage at the end of the row. He's sitting against the corner, holding himself sideways, as if he's been punched in the ribs and it still hurts. I call out to Sandy, "What's wrong with him?"

"That's Blueberry. Berry for short." Sandy comes closer to tell me more. "She hatched out fine, but then something happened that none of us saw. Radiographs show a spinal fracture."

"Can't you re-fracture it and put her in a brace?"

"No, Tom already asked about it."

Berry watches us. She listens, too, her head tilted, fixed on mine. "Is she in pain?" I ask Sandy.

"Probably not. She eats just fine, and she is growing, though slower than we'd like."

"What about physical therapy?"

"Do you know how?"

"Well, you have to keep the muscles and tendons flexible to help with healing. When my dad hurt his wrist he went every day for a month and he was fine afterward."

"If you know what to do, I think you should see if it works on her."

We feed the rest of the babies and then get the food for the big ones. They are all tuned in to the schedule. Even the shy ones are waiting near the places where we put down food, and once we step back, they move in and eat, grabbing chunks of banana first.

When all the lizards are fed, Sandy goes to be with Digger and I walk to Berry's cage. Her siblings are basking in sun that's pouring in on one side. Berry leans against the wooden frame, and I look at her C-shaped body while she peers up at me.

After a minute I open the door, and she starts to pull herself around in a circle. Easing my fingers under her belly, I lift just a little so her feet are still on the cage floor, and with my other hand I grasp her spine between my thumb and fingers and try to straighten her body. It doesn't seem to be hurting. I apply more pressure and then she's standing and I take away my hands. Her body rocks a little, and she takes a step before tipping over onto her side, with her back in its C shape again.

I cup her in the palm of my hand and lift her up. "We're going to work together," I say. She tilts her head and looks at my face, where the words came from. With my thumb I rub her back and arms and legs. I feel her warm skin like raw silk. Again it registers that I'm touching a lizard, a totally new experience for me. Shifting her around in my hand, I rotate her limbs, first one way and then the other. I take her body in both hands and gently pull, straightening the spine, and I hold to the count of ten. I remember watching Dad do something like this with his injured wrist. I repeat the exercise ten times. Berry doesn't struggle, but I keep a close watch in case there's a change that might tell me if she's in pain. I'm so involved I don't hear the footsteps behind me.

"Hi, there," says a voice. Startled, I turn and see a tall man with blue eyes wearing a faded BIRP shirt and khaki trousers. His face is sunburned and rough, as though he had a skin problem long ago.

"Tom," he says, putting out his hand.

Berry is resting in my right hand, so I give Tom my left.

"Sorry I couldn't be here yesterday. I had a meeting in town. Negotiating for more land. For these guys." He nods at Berry. "It would be great if we could get this one straightened out. Pun intended."

"I'd like to try."

"Let me know if there's anything you need for that." His cell phone rings and he checks it, then asks, "Did Sandy mention the tour groups?"

"She said I'd be on my own with feeding while she did them."

"That's right. Visitors make donations and tell folks back home about the blue iguana, and more donations come. So the deal is, we're tourist-friendly."

"If Sandy's not here, who does the tour?"

"Whoever's least occupied."

"I'll try, but I don't know anything about the iguanas."

"Sure you do. You're working with head-start babies, you know what they eat, how old they are, and why we're head-starting them. You know why they're endangered. It's your first day and you're already giving one of them physical therapy."

Again he looks at Berry resting in my hand. In that moment I see more than his dedication to the iguanas. I see his love for them.

"Don't worry," he says. "Odds are you won't ever have to do the tour." He checks his watch. "Lunchtime."

At the Mess Sandy has put out bread and stuff for making sandwiches. She and Tom fix ham sandwiches and I make one with lettuce, tomato, mustard, and sliced pickle. Tom brings a bag of potato chips to the table while Sandy gets paper towels for napkins. She says to Tom, "Clarice needs BIRP shirts."

His mouth full, Tom nods. He finishes lunch in what seems like three bites, gets up, pours himself coffee, and says, "They're in my office."

I follow Tom, and the first thing I see is a .22 in the corner behind the desk. On the floor by a bookshelf are a couple of boxes, one stuffed with T-shirts, the other with postcards.

"Large okay?"

"Yes."

While Tom finds the shirts I look at photos pinned to the wall of people I figure must be volunteers. Some hold iguanas. Most are sunburned and scratched up like they tumbled downhill through a patch of briars. I recognize Meg and Josh. Then I see a terrible photo and my lunch turns to acid in my stomach. It's a shriveled carcass of an iguana. The caption says, *1991. The iguana apparently died* in the trap set by a farmer to protect his newly planted pump-kins and yams, and his body was later slung aside.

"You okay?" Tom holds T-shirts in one hand.

"How could anyone do such a thing?" I stare at the photo.

"If you're hungry, you'll do what you think you have to in order to protect your food."

I look at Tom, trying to sort out my feelings about what he just said. He finds an empty cardboard box for the shirts. "You've got one of each color," he says.

"Can I buy a postcard? I need to write my brother."

"Which one do you like?"

"The one of Digger."

"That's Yellow." Tom takes a bunch of cards and puts them in the box. "Compliments of BIRP."

"Thank you."

"What's your brother's size?"

"He's a little guy."

"Medium?"

"Perfect."

He pulls out a gray T-shirt. "When you need to mail something, leave it in the out box by the door and it'll go when one of us makes it to the post office." Again Tom checks his watch. "Got a call to make before Timothy gets here."

After we put away the lunch things Sandy and I go out on the porch with a bowl of green beans to stem. The moment we sit, Macho comes trotting over, his long tail clearing the ground, then touching back down as he slows and comes to rest just a few feet in front of us.

"I can't get over these lizards," I say.

Macho watches Sandy. She tosses a bean and he chomps it down.

"I mean, not only do they look like dinosaurs, they're just so *different*. With a cat or dog, you talk to them and pet them and they purr or wag their tails. You pretty much know how they feel. But these guys are mysterious. It makes me want to find out more, to really *know* them. Does that make sense?"

"Sure it does."

Suddenly Macho drops his belly and raises his head, eyes wide and fixed on the gate. There's a sound of tires on gravel and a cloud of white dust as a red pickup pulls in, sun-faded like the BIRP truck.

"It's Timothy. He's going to help Tom with that dead tree."

A slim West Indian guy in khaki trousers and a DIVE CAYMAN shirt steps onto the porch.

"Clarice, this is Timothy," Sandy says. "He's a year ahead of me at GCIU. Marine bio."

We shake hands. "You've come to work with the iguanas?" he asks.

"Yeah, to see if I can help."

"She's doing physical therapy on Blueberry," Sandy says. "The two-year-old with the spinal problem?"

"That's great."

Tom comes out and puts his hands on his waist in a way that says it's time to get to work.

"I managed to get the Stihl running," Timothy tells him.

"Let's try it out," Tom says.

They go through the parking area and into the bush behind the Mess. Sandy and I keep snapping beans while the whiny buzz of the saw starts and stops.

"It's funny to hear a chainsaw when it's not for firewood."

"Four years later, we're just finishing the cleanup from Ivan."

"Oh, the hurricane."

"What a disaster. So many people left homeless. Trees down everywhere. In some places everything green was wiped out. If not for the bald palms still standing, you'd think it was November in the northeastern part of the States."

"That's terrible. I'm afraid to ask about the iguanas."

"You know what? We didn't lose *one*. Downed trees blocked the roads, and it took three days to cut our way through. When we finally got in, iguanas were swimming in their pens and resting on fallen branches, but they all made it."

"Thank goodness." I toss Macho a bean. "How did this guy get his name?"

Sandy grins. "He courts at least three of the park's females . . . that we know about."

The saw buzz stops. Soon there are footsteps on the porch. Timothy sits down on the steps nearby and wipes sweat from his forehead. "Macho," he says, "are these girls keeping you full of beans?"

Tom goes inside and returns with a frosty-looking

bottle of ginger ale for Timothy. "I'm going fishing," he says. "You folks enjoy the rest of the day. Tim, see you in a few weeks. Have a good trip and say hi to Mom."

Timothy raises the ginger ale in a gesture of cheers. "See you then." He says to me, "We're having a little dinner party, if you'd like to come. It's my grandmother's seventy-fifth birthday."

"Sure, sounds great."

He says, "It will be a traditional island dinner, with johnnycakes, and peas and rice. And we'll have lobsters."

I feel my smile fade away. The last time I was at a restaurant I had to run for the bathroom when they brought out a whole boiled lobster. Sandy says, "Clarice is vegan."

Timothy shrugs. "My avocados will be ready to pick. And I can ask Dad to leave the salt pork out of the peas and rice."

"I'm hungry already," Sandy says, picking up the bowls. She opens the screen door and goes inside. Resting my chin on my knee, I reach down to push a few stem ends that missed the bowl into a neat pile.

Timothy says, "Did I say something wrong?"

"When people eat lobsters they boil them alive."

"Not me. I kill them first."

"How?"

"With a knife, here." He puts the side of his hand to his forehead, above and between his eyes, which are hazel.

"The biology teacher in our school did that to a frog."

"Oh, pithing. It's not right."

"But isn't that what you're doing to the lobster?"

"Yes and no. I'm not trying to keep the lobster alive to observe nervous responses. I'm trying to kill him as quickly as possible. And whereas the frog has a highly developed central nervous system, the lobster does not. Still, they should be killed before you cook them."

I blink. "You should be the biology teacher."

He nods. "It's nice of you to say."

"The way they do biology in school, it's like the animals are machines that don't feel pain or fear, and that's not true."

"I agree. So your approach to biology is more philosophical. What's your major?"

"I'm still in high school. I'm supposed to be applying to college, but I just want to be with animals."

"My mother would be interested in your work with the injured iguana. She's a veterinarian."

"Wow, that's so cool. I'm not smart enough. I mean, I don't have the academic skills, and they say vet school is hard. Besides, I'm not sure I want to work in an office. Actually, I feel kind of stuck."

Inside, a phone rings.

"I don't know why I'm telling you this. It's boring."

"No, it's not. But you're right about veterinary school."

"That was Mary," Sandy says through the kitchen window. "She can't gather food tomorrow, so we'll do it."

Timothy stands, arching his back to stretch. "Time to go help Dad with the boat. I hope you'll come to the party."

"I will. Definitely."

"Later, Tim," Sandy calls out.

He gets in his truck and drives out the gate. Shade from the porch roof has reached Macho, and he moves to be in the sun. I lean against the post. There are sounds of cooking from inside, the sizzling of chopped vegetables going into a hot pan, the clank of a lid. I should go help. The walls of the iguana pens are turning pinkish orange in the afternoon light, and I can just make out the names on the little wooden signs. Digger, Elle Woods. Sara, Jessica, Eldemire. I feel Macho looking at me from his patch of sun.

Tires crunch gravel as the BIRP truck pulls in. Meg and Josh climb out with beach towels around their necks. Meg's shirt has wet patches shaped like a bikini top.

"You guys went swimming."

"The ocean's divine," Meg says. "What are you up to?"

"Just hanging. I was about to go help with dinner."

Sandy comes out with a beer in hand. "Got it under control."

"Time for a shower?" Josh asks.

"Plenty."


When we sit down to eat, I tell Sandy, "Thanks for doing it like this." She made a stir-fry of the green beans and peppers and onions, with chicken cooked on the side.

We dig in, hungry. I say, "So, what did you guys do? I know you were out in the Salina, but what's it like? The work, I mean."

Josh looks at the ceiling. "Imagine trudging over razor-sharp rock through thorny scrub with hot sun pounding on your head, a fresh maiden plum rash welling up on your arm, and sweat dripping in your eyes while you try to read the tracking device. Don't forget the huge blister forming on your heel."

Meg rolls her eyes. "It was a glorious day. Seriously, we got some good data."

"But what *is* the data? I know you make observations, but how do you know what to write down? Sorry to ask so many dumb questions, but I'm trying to figure it out."

"Come with us tomorrow and see for yourself," Josh says.

"We're picking food. The day after?"

"You're on," Meg says. "And just wait till you see a blue in the wild."

It's dusk when we say good night, but I'm wide awake and don't want to be inside just yet. I sit on the edge of the Mess porch. Now the pen walls glow white against the darkness of the trees beyond, and I wonder if Macho goes there to sleep.

Something makes me turn. The black cat is frozen in his tracks, watching me. And I see that he is a she, in desperate need of brushing. I remember reading that the angora was bred as a parlor cat, to like sitting on a lap, having her long, silky fur stroked. "And look where you are now, kitty," I say. Her eyes widen and she bolts for the bushes. I go inside and get a chicken wing from dinner, and when I come back she is crouched at the edge of the yard. I toss the wing and she flinches, but then she comes forward, grabs the meat, and disappears.

I get a towel from my room and walk to the showers. The fluorescent light is drawing in bugs, and on the ceiling are two geckos. One snaps up a moth. A bat swoops in and then back out through one of the window openings.

In the mirror my face is pink. Not exactly tan, but it's a start. When I turn on the shower, a pale spider the size of a silver dollar runs across the concrete floor and stops at the doorway, as if deciding whether or not to leave. Like the geckos and the bat, she's hunting bugs attracted by the light. Joe would be thrilled by this place.

Back in my room I sit at the desk and take out a post-card and write:

*Dear Joe,*

*My first day on the job was great! And you wouldn't believe the spider I saw in the shower just now. She was fast, but she held still long enough for me to get a good look. She was the same white as the sand, with eight shiny eyes and—*

I stop. Joe will be upset about a spider in a bathroom unless I explain that she wasn't trapped in there. Mom has tried to pull him away from spiders in public bathrooms, and it's impossible: he anchors himself and won't budge. It's better to just help him collect the spider to take outside, even when people are watching like you're completely nuts. The thing is, I get how Joe feels. When I see a spider in a public bathroom I cringe and feel like, *Ugh! The poor thing.* I think about the spider being washed away in soapy disinfectant when someone cleans. But there are usually other women in there and I can't just go chasing a spider around, creating a commotion.

So I write that I helped the spider get out. I close the letter with: *I miss you. Love, Clarice. P.S. I hope you like the shirt. It's from Tom, the director.*

I fiddle with the pen. My journal sits on the desk, and after a minute I open it. The last entry is Tufty, with the little hearts. I turn the page and draw Berry with her stomach that's round, because of the way she holds herself, and then I draw hearts around her, too.

One of the geckos is on the ceiling, right above me. I make a sketch of him with his big eyes. When I'm finished, I close the journal and go sit on my bed. Leaning against the cool cinderblock, I feel the air coming in the screen door like a warm bath. The slightly salty smell reminds me that the ocean isn't far.

Early in the morning Sandy and I carry buckets of food and our cups of coffee out to the head-start cages. By the time the tour group arrives, we're in the Jeep with a cooler full of water bottles and sandwiches for lunch. We have on khaki trousers and sneakers and BIRP shirts, though Sandy has gotten creative with this last one: the sleeves are cut off and it's cropped to almost show her belly button. When she reaches for the seat belt, I catch a glimpse of a tiny gold ring. I think about this group of girls back home who went to get their navels pierced for graduation. They'll be off to college this year.

"Is Timothy the guy you were going out with?" I ask her.

She smiles and says no.

"So how did he get involved with BIRP?"

"His dad, Willy, is an old fishing buddy of Tom's. Tim actually keeps pretty busy, helping Willy with the boat and diving on the reef. Chasing fish instead of girls."

My face feels hot and I get out the sunscreen. "Tom didn't seem thrilled about doing the tour."

"He just likes to grumble."

"Is he married?"

"He was, ages ago. From what I gather, it didn't end well, and I think he kind of fled the States. He didn't bail on responsibilities, though. I know he's got a son he put through college. But he's been alone ever since."

"That's sad."

"Tom is doing fine. BIRP is his baby. He hates the paperwork, but it gets done, and then he gets to go fishing. What could be bad?"

"I guess. Meg and Josh seem happy."

"They make a good team." Sandy pulls onto the side of the road and stops the engine. It's quiet except for the chirping of little birds. There's a break in the forest as if a fire opened it up long ago. Some of the trees are just starting to come back. I shield my eyes and scan the area. The only tree I recognize is thatch palm.

We take laundry sacks and make our way into the field. Sandy squats to pick some weeds that look sort of like nettles, only not as tall. "This is jackswitch," she says. "It's one of the staples in the iguanas' diet."

I see how she pinches off the top parts and I get busy picking. After a while we move deeper into the field, where more trees have come up. Sandy walks around one without touching the dark, shiny leaves that remind me of Mom's wisteria. "This is maiden plum."

"The stuff Josh got on his arm?"

"Uh-huh."

Near a group of thatch palms we find a mass of what I think is trumpet vine, except the flowers are white instead of orange. "Whitewood flowers," Sandy says. "Iguanas adore them."

We gather most of the blossoms, and Sandy shows me other plants to pick. Our sacks fill as we move about the area, a little talk, a little quiet, with the birds flitting from tree to bush. It makes me think of picking blueberries with my mom. I ask, "How many kinds of plants will they eat?"

"At least a hundred. There are a lot more they don't."

"Because they're poisonous?"

"What they will and won't eat is about nutrition. They go for the ones that are digestible, and that have more protein."

I'm about to ask how iguanas know when I see a small blue lizard race up the tree right behind Sandy. I point and she turns and grabs him off the trunk. Thrashing side to side he whips his skinny tail, desperately trying to get free. My heart races as I consider what it must be like to be snatched up by some gigantic creature.

"Grand Cayman anole," she says. "Want to have a look?" She holds the lizard out to me, but I'm frozen.

"He's terrified. Can we let him go?"

Sandy opens her hand near the tree. The lizard hops on and scurries up the trunk, then looks down at us with his bead eyes. "He's not *that* terrified."

"He's in shock."

In a burst the anole runs the rest of the way to the top and disappears. I look into the darkness at the core of the frond bundle and imagine him pressed in, motionless, except for his tiny ribs heaving in and out.

"I need water," I say, and go to the Jeep to get some.


Back at the Mess we put our sacks in the fridge with the blue sign, but not before taking out some whitewood flowers. When Sandy climbs over the pen wall, Digger comes running.

"There's my boy!" She holds out a flower and he eats it in one bite. She gives him another, and another, until they're gone. He tilts his head to look at her.

"You ate them all up, honey," she says, scratching his back. He jacks himself up like a cat.

I think, *Wow, is he blue*, and I say, "Sandy? Is Digger more blue today?"

She scoops him up in her arms. "Oh, yes, he's just so excited."

"Wait—he's more blue because he's excited?"

"Yeah, they're blue when they want to be."

"How does that work? What makes them want to change color?"

"To see each other better. And when they don't want to be seen, the blue fades to gray, like the rocks. If they're cold, the blue really fades."

Digger pushes himself up in Sandy's arms and looks over the grounds as if surveying his kingdom. He is charged and alive, his red eyes alert, head and shoulders brilliant.

Sandy nuzzles his neck. "Don't quote me on this, but I think they turn extra blue when they're happy."


I go to Berry with my hand full of flowers. As I pass Billy's pen I see him on his rock, watching me. I stop. "Billy?"

He lifts his head. I stand at the wall and take a flower from the crumpled bouquet and hold it out, turning it slowly so the petals fall over each other. After a moment he climbs down and comes to me. He stops an arm's length away and looks into my eyes, and again I catch my breath. It's unsettling, yet I'm drawn to him.

I stretch out my arm, offering the flower. Billy snags one of the petals with his tongue and pulls the whole flower into his jaws, where it disappears. I can't see teeth, but then I remember the scar on Sandy's thumb. I give Billy the flowers one by one and it's like when I was six years old and got to feed cubes of sugar to old Mr. Taft's horse. I walk back and tell Sandy, "Billy ate the flowers and I need some for Berry."

"See that path behind the last pen?" She points to a line of trees and bushes at the edge of the grounds. "It goes to the Botanic Park. There's a hedgerow of hibiscus. We're supposed to leave them for visitors, but I pick for Digger all the time."

I walk down the path and see the hibiscus hedge that Sandy was talking about. Once I've got a bunch of the big yellow flowers, I head back to Berry's cage. Her eyes find mine as if making a quick identification. Then she sees the flowers and works at pulling herself to me. Berry's eyes are not as red as Billy's, and she isn't very blue, but only some of the babies are. I figure it's because they need to stay camouflaged. I give her cage mates a few so they won't try to steal hers while she eats, and I tuck one in my pocket for after physical therapy. I've handled her only once, and already she's acting as though she expects it.

I do the routine—I massage her back and limbs and finish with a stretch, straightening her spine and holding to the count of ten. She doesn't seem to be in pain. I set her down in the cage and she doesn't want to let go; she holds on and leans into my hand. I take the flower from my pocket and give it to her.

I stay like that, leaning against the cage door cradling Berry, feeling the way she fills my hand with her warm little body that needs help. My throat tightens, and I think of how Joe's hand feels in mine, and I hold Berry until my arm is numb and my feet are sore from standing too long.

. . .

"So are we on for tomorrow?" Josh asks, loading his burrito with hot sauce. I made a pot of black beans and we found tortillas in the freezer. Sandy roasted them on the stovetop while Meg made a salsa of tomatoes, lime juice, and green chili peppers.

"I want to, but I'm afraid I'll slow you guys down."

"That's not going to happen."

"It's just that I'm totally inexperienced."

Meg says, "We didn't have experience at first."

"Go," Sandy says.

They're all looking at me.

"Okay." I can't keep from smiling. "I'll go."

Later I write in my journal about Billy and the way he looks at me. I write about Berry, too, and how different her look is. I try to make drawings of their faces, adjusting the shape of the eyelids to get the right expression. Both are curious, but Billy is more so. Berry's focus is safety.

I turn the page and write about picking flowers and leaves. I make sketches of plants from memory, and then I make a drawing of the anole, with his spots and eyes like beads, and it occurs to me that I'm always drawing animal eyes. I put down my pen and reach up to rub my stiff neck. A gecko waddles up the wall close by. Maybe he's losing his fear of me. I'm tempted to touch him, but I know he'll run away, so I just watch to see what he will do. His skin looks soft and fragile, almost translucent. He's thin-skinned. Like me.

Tomorrow I'll see a blue iguana in the wild. I can hardly believe it—me, barely passing biology, going out there with field biologists. I turn off the light and get into bed, but I can't sleep. I keep thinking I should see if the alarm clock is set.

There's a tap on the door. "Clarice?"

I stumble around in the dark and get the door open. It's Meg and a nice smell of coffee. "We're going to the Salina." She hands me the coffee.

"Mm, thanks." I take the cup and drink some. "I'm sorry I overslept."

"Meet us at the truck as soon as you can."

"I'll be right there." I splash water on my face, get dressed, and grab an energy bar on my way out.

"Morning!" Josh says when I get there. "We're going to have an excellent day, I can feel it." He looks at my feet. "You can't wear those."

"I only wear these. They're leather-free."

"No good. You need boots with tough soles and ankle support."

"I wore these when Sandy and I went picking."

"This is different. We're hiking into rough territory."

"I've got an extra pair," Meg says, and takes off running before I can protest.

"Nothing else will hold up on that karst," Josh tells me. "You *will* slow us down if your shoes fall apart." He climbs into the bed of the truck and checks a black nylon bag of what must be some kind of equipment.

Meg returns, a little out of breath. "I bet we're nearly the same size."

I look at the leather boots with their laces hanging down.

"You're not supporting a product of cruelty," she says. "I was the one who bought them."

When she holds out the boots I know I need to put them on. I take them and say, "Thank you."

The sky is glowing in the east and we're on our way, Josh driving. I wriggle my toes inside the boots, which fit fine. Mom and Dad would be proud.

Meg shifts in her seat to face me. "We've been tracking and recording movements of twenty iguanas. I'll show you how the radio equipment works and we'll trap an iguana so you can see how we process them."

My shoulders go up. "It sounds so traumatic."

"We need to show how the head-start iguanas are doing," Josh says. "Which means we need to weigh them and take measurements. Also, we need to track their movement in the zone."

Meg says, "We have to show that the iguanas need a specific acreage for a sustainable population so we can negotiate for land grants."

"If these guys are eating plants, why so much space?"

Josh catches my eye in the rearview mirror. "When there's overcrowding, subordinate males can't establish territories and attract mates. Their chances of siring young go down, and that represents genetic loss."

"Speaking of genes, we've been trying to locate GRG's nest," Meg says.

"GRG?"

"Green-Red-Green. A wild female they tagged in April."

"So I'm guessing you want to collect her eggs and head-start the babies."

"Right. So few wild blues are left, and we need their progeny to expand the gene pool."

The sun is just above the tree line when we pull off the road and park. It's already getting hot as we heft our backpacks full of water bottles and equipment and start down a path into the bush. I realize I forgot my sunscreen.

"This is a dry thorn forest. Xerophytic shrubland," Josh says over his shoulder.

None of the trees are tall or very leafy, like in the forest back home. I see a spiny plant as thick as my arm and I have to stop. "I've never seen a cactus outside of a clay pot." I shake my head and keep going.

Meg says, "These things coming up at the edge of the path are flower spikes from the banana orchid. We don't really have topsoil here, but there are patches of what's called oxisol. A lot of these plants have evolved to grow in it."

It is pricklier here than where Sandy and I gathered food, and there's a lot more of the rocky stuff they call karst. I have to watch my step.

"Be sure your boots are laced up tight," Meg says.

"Yeah, now I get it about the shoes."

A warm wind passes through, making the palm

fronds clatter. After a while we come to an area clear of scrub, with trees that create a dappled shade. "Base camp," Josh says, unloading his pack.

I see some cagelike things. Traps.

"I'm going to get tracking," Meg says, lifting the antenna, which looks like a four-foot-tall aluminum crucifix with two extra cross pieces. A thin cord connects it to a receiver that she holds out. "Clarice, this tells me the iguana's approximate location. Then I use binoculars to see him, or her, and I record the colors of the beads on the crest, and the coordinates of the sighting. If we need data on that particular animal, we set a trap."

"What's giving the antenna signals?"

"A radio transmitter. It looks like a tadpole glued on just above the hind legs." Meg gets a water bottle and puts it in her shoulder bag. "Good luck, guys," she says, heading into the bush with the antenna out in front.

Josh picks up a trap. "Let's catch an iguana."

Not far from base camp we come to a huge outcropping of karst.

"We'll get RYB," Josh says. "She can't resist ripe banana."

"Let me guess: Red-Yellow-Blue."

"Yep. Also known as Rib." Josh sets the trap and we're walking back to camp when I hear something and stop.

"What?"

"Something metal—claws on metal."

We go back and there's a big iguana in the trap.

"Wiggly Worm!"

"The one that bit Meg?"

"Yes, he's a devil. We call him Wiggly, because he wiggles out of traps."

Wiggly claws the screen and I cover my ears. I see the awful photo in Tom's office. Josh reaches in and grabs Wiggly. His mouth is wide open, and he lashes his tail and struggles. My heart thumps in my chest.

"Whoa, Wiggly," Josh says. "You restrain them like this." Josh holds the lizard around the neck and shoulders with one hand and around the legs and tail base with the other.

Wiggly's jaws are still wide open and I can see the neat rows of teeth. Josh tightens his grip as the lizard writhes and hisses and lashes his tail. Then suddenly he stops and his eyes are sunken, as if he's pulled them in. His jaws shut, almost, and he goes limp.

"I really, really think we should let him go," I say. "This is intensely cruel. He thinks he's going to die."

Josh's eyes meet mine and he gives Wiggly to me. "If you hold him I can get measurements. Don't worry, the fight's gone out of him, mostly."

I take Wiggly and hold him the way Josh showed me. Somehow it helps me calm down. Josh gets the clipboard and other things out of the backpack. I see Wiggly's beads on the wire through his crest and think how much it had to hurt going in. I try to comfort him by stroking his belly with my forefinger. His tail twitches and his red eyes glare into mine and he opens his jaws a little more. I stop petting him and my eyes well up. Wiggly's tail relaxes and his jaws shut. I try to tell him I'm sorry with my eyes.

"We verify identity," Josh says. "The beads check out, the PIT tag matches."

"What's a PIT tag?"

"Passive Integrated Transponder. It's like he's got his own barcode just under the skin." Josh writes down the information. Then he measures Wiggly from the tip of his nose to his tail base. "SVL stands for snout-vent length. Wiggly is 32.5 cm, SVL. His tail is 37.5. You check him for missing toenails, scars, and any other signs of injury. Note his pelvic girdle: Is it thin, can you see bones? In Wiggly's case, no, he's in great shape."

Josh's cell beeps. "Yeah? We're on our way." He stuffs the cell back in his pocket. "Meg's located GRG."

Wiggly pushes against my hands, scraping my skin raw with his scaly heels. "Can we let him go now?"

"One more measurement." Josh unfolds a cloth sack. "He'll get over it in two seconds."

He doesn't struggle as Josh bags him and gets his weight. "One point five kilos."

I finish filling in the data sheet. It's preprinted with little boxes and lines so that all you have to do is write in numbers.

"If we wanted to track him we'd glue on a transmitter. But we're good on Wiggly for now." Josh puts the sack down and opens it. Wiggly steps out and looks at us. He blinks and then trots into the bush in no particular hurry.

We catch up with Meg and she's got her binoculars aimed at something in the distance. "Look," she says, handing them to Josh.

"Oh, man. She's something. Where are your eggs, missy?" He gives me the binoculars and points. "Just there, under the buttonwood, on the rock."

In the green and gray and brown of the forest I find a patch of brilliant blue, and I focus on it. I hold my breath. I remember what Sandy said about the iguanas being blue when they want to be. A pang goes through my chest—a longing for this iguana to live out her life exactly as she is, undisturbed by people.

I give the binoculars back to Meg. "I guess we better find those eggs."

The moment we walk into what might be GRG's nesting area she disappears among the rocks. We each take a patch of ground and search. I don't have a clue how an iguana thinks.

After an hour Josh is exasperated. "The nest could be anywhere. Maybe it doesn't exist."

"She's been staying close, right in this area." Meg outlines a circle by pointing to a tree, an agave, and the outcropping of karst.

I squat and put my palms against the earth. It feels solid, with a powdery-crusty layer of soil that's only an inch or two deep. I get down on my knees and make sweeping arcs with both hands, trying to feel for changes in the ground. After a while I stand and go closer to the rocks where GRG was basking. I see a mark in the oxisol, a line that could have been made by a lizard tail. Again I kneel and search with my hands. "Wait," I say, almost to myself.

"What?"

"Maybe something."

They both come and look.

"It feels as though the ground is less dense here."

Kneeling, Josh and Meg run their hands over the surface. "Yes," Meg says, "let's dig here. Carefully."

Soon we break through into a sort of trench. "It's the entry to the chamber," Josh says.

We dig eagerly, cautiously, and then I'm reaching into the ground, up to my elbow. My fingers touch something and there's no question. "Found it," I say, and pull my hand out. "That was an egg, I'm positive."

Meg and Josh sit up straight. We look at each other and then we're all smiling. We bury the nest entry and make a small pile of rocks at the site. Meg writes notes on her map. "Tom will be thrilled."


That night, scratched up and sunburned, we climb into the Jeep and head up the road toward Johnny's. I ask Sandy how the day went.

"I gave Billy a banana and told him it was from the pretty girl with long brown hair. Tell you what, he's definitely more interested in people since you came."

"I'm not sure that's a good thing."

"Oh, it's great for the tours when the big guys sit up on their rocks all glorious and blue."

"And Berry?"

"She missed you."

"She did? How could you tell?"

"Well, I opened the cage door and put in the food and she just looked at me."

"Waiting for therapy?"

"Yes, the contact, I imagine. Wow, the place is packed," Sandy says, driving into the parking area.

We get the last table for four. The smell of fried food makes my mouth water. They order beers and grouper sandwiches and I get a salad and fries and pineapple juice. When the drinks come Josh makes a toast. "To GRG's eggs, thanks to Clarice."

"Thanks to you guys for getting me out there."

He says, "You should find a school with a strong biology program."

"I walked out of biology when the teacher pithed a frog. I'm not going back."

"That's too bad, because you could do this work, and help make a difference."

I peel off a bit of the label on the ketchup bottle. "Any of us could've found the nest."

"Maybe. I've worked with biologists who are so pragmatic they treat animals like specimens. You do have to record data precisely, but you also have to be tuned in to the animals. I know it was hard for you to process Wiggly, but you were right there the whole time."

"He's right," Sandy says. "I've seen you with Berry and the others."

"I did like being out there."

"Listen, I hated the frog thing too, but it's part of the deal," Sandy says. "Actually, you can request alternatives to dissection. They don't make it easy, but you can."

We're quiet, tired and maybe hypnotized by the flickering candle in the jar. The food comes and we put on tartar sauce, ketchup, oil and vinegar. I'm eating fries three at a time. "Oh my God, these are amazing."

"Fieldwork makes food amazing," Josh says. He bites into his sandwich and I'm shocked at myself for finding the smell delicious—the warm butter and lemon and herbs on the broiled fish, the toasted bun. Then I catch a glimpse of the white cooked flesh and I pick up my fork and dig into my salad. It's got little cherry tomatoes and cucumbers and shredded purple cabbage, plus there's spinach in with the lettuce. Salad never tasted so good, Josh is right.

After scarfing down veggies and more fries I come up for air and find my napkin. "Can I ask how you two met?"

"In the pre-vet program at Cal Poly. We both started out wanting to be veterinarians. I was in the bovine unit and Josh was in poultry, but we drifted over to the herp department and kept bumping into each other."

"You were following me," Josh says.

"You were always in the turtle room with the herp dweebs, playing with the baby *sulcatas*."

"Well, they were cute."

"Anyway, on a date at the San Diego Zoo we found out about BIRP. This is our third year."

"So what will you guys do, keep coming back? I mean, how will you make a living?"

Josh takes a long drink of beer. "We've entrenched ourselves in the university system. Fieldwork is part of our doctoral studies. With the degrees we'll be able to write research proposals, get funding, and also teach."

"It's scary and makes my head hurt. I'm so *not* academic."

Meg says, "Pass the classes and get out in the field."

"Maybe I could work in a zoo. Be a keeper or something."

"You could. At least two zoos in the States are working with blues."

Sandy says, "Yeah, the Gladys Porter Zoo had one who was sixty-nine when he died. Godzilla."

"We're talking, like, people years, not dog years?"

"That's right."

"Incredible."

The waiter asks if we want another round. "Thanks, just the check," Sandy says.

Josh finishes his beer and sets the bottle down. "Whatever you decide to do, Clarice, you'll pull it off. Field research has my vote."

Sandy pays the bill and we walk out to the Jeep.


Back in my room I draw Wiggly, and write about how he got his name. Not WGW, but Wiggly Worm, so bursting with life it takes my breath away. He could live for sixty years. I try to picture an old, wrinkly iguana. On the opposite page I make a sketch of GRG basking on a rock. Even though I don't have a blue-colored pencil, I draw her so she looks happy, and I do it without giving her a smile.

A breeze moves the window screen and I glance at the clock. I get out the paper and envelopes and write, *Dear Mom and Dad.* I tell them what it's like here, and about the people I've met. I tell them I got a little sunburned out in the bush, and that I had to wear leather boots and it's fine, and I'm fine—great, in fact. But don't expect me to come home and eat a cheeseburger. I draw a smiley face after that and close the letter, *Love, Clarice.* Then I write, *P.S. Thanks for buying my ticket down here. I hope I can figure out what to do with my life.*

I get a lump in my throat and put down my pen. It's great that Josh thinks I could be a field biologist, but I don't see how. A gecko is on the windowsill, hunting. Drawn by the desk light, moths have gathered on the other side of the screen. I haven't had the chance to see him so close, and I notice that the edges of his mouth curve up slightly. His pale pink tongue slips out to clean his eye. I fold my arms on the desk and rest my head so I can watch him.

At dawn the birds in the gumbo-limbo tree sing like the sun is rising for the first time ever. I dress quickly. On my way to the Mess I see the cat crouched under a bush, watching me. It's my fault she's getting bolder, letting herself be seen. *Run away from here, kitty.*

The Mess has a coffee-and-toast aroma that makes me hungry the moment I step inside. Sandy pokes her head out of the office. "We're in here."

I pour myself coffee and go in. "Morning," Tom says.

He has papers in his hand and sets them down. "There were ten nice eggs in that nest."

"You got them already?"

"Yep. Had just enough light. Let's keep up the good work. And with luck we'll be set to make our case by the end of summer."

"For more land."

Sandy puts her hand on a thick folder. "The BIRP Plan."

Tom leans back in his chair. "We've got a hundred eggs incubating and that many ready for release this year."

"Two hundred? That should save them from going extinct."

"Hardly—it'll take more like a thousand. Even then, there are dangers. Dogs and cats will continue to be a serious problem until we can get them under control."

I swallow hard. Sandy says, "Come see the eggs."

"Aren't they buried in something?"

"Tupperware."

The room across from the office is warm and there's a fan gently moving air. The Tupperware boxes are lined up on a table, each with a name and date written on masking tape with a Sharpie. Sandy touches one with "GRG 2008" written on it, and points to me. I wish I'd been there to help dig up the eggs and see them go in that box. She lifts the lid on another, labeled "2008, Sire: Digger. Dam: Elle Woods." Nestled in Pearlite are eleven eggs the size of a chicken's.

"Digger's babies," she whispers.

I wait for her to put the lid back before I say quietly, "They're huge. How can they fit inside?"

"The shells are leathery. They fill up every bit of space and press against the organs, leaving no room for food. That's why Sara and the other breeding females are so thin. But they'll gain the weight back. It just takes a while."

Tom opens the door. "Got a busy day ahead. Sandy's giving a tour at eleven, so you're on your own with the feeding. And that group from the Reptile Club is coming."

"I'll help you get started," Sandy says.

We take out the sacks of leaves and flowers and I start chopping fruit. "What's the Reptile Club?"

"Every summer they come for a few days and do a project. This year they're building head-start cages. When the eggs hatch, we'll need every single one."


Little pairs of eyes watch me as I work. When the cage door shuts, the babies climb down off the screen and rush over to eat. They're learning that human hands bring food, but they'll have to forget about that one day. I get an image of them going free—a hundred little ones fanning out, running over leaf litter and karst, around cacti and up trees.

I hear Sandy coming closer. She is telling the tour group about how the baby iguanas will gain their ability to turn bluer as they mature. "And the red sclera of their eyes will show much more," she says.

The group is small, four adults and three kids. The girl is quiet, looking at the iguanas. She's maybe nine and holds a plush toy I think is an alligator. I can hardly tell for sure, it's so faded and misshapen, no doubt from being hugged and kissed many, many times. One of the grown-ups is occupied with a toddler, while a boy Joe's age starts running with his arms out like an airplane. It's making me edgy and too distracted to open cage doors safely, so I wait with my hands in my pockets.

"Our amazing volunteer," Sandy says, making me smile. "These baby iguanas get special care every day, and it's a lot of work! Our volunteers go out picking fresh wild plants and flowers to feed these hungry little ones. In two years each iguana will receive his or her own colored beads and PIT tag so that our volunteers in the field can keep an eye on them once they are free. And one day, we hope the blue iguana will survive on his own."

I like how Sandy emphasizes *volunteer*, to get them to make a donation. Suddenly the boy runs up to a cage and whacks the screen, making the babies scatter and climb the cage walls. Sandy goes to him. "Why do you want the iguanas to be afraid of you?" He turns to listen. Her eyes widen. "They need to eat their breakfast, so they can grow up to be wild blue dragons of the island bush!"

The boy is still. Sandy grins. "Now," she says, "shall we go see the big ones?"

She leads the group away, but the quiet girl has stayed behind, looking at a group of two-year-olds. They are watching her too.

"Got your alligator friend there?" I ask.

"Crocodile." She puts her hand against the screen. The babies are alert, but they don't scatter.

The mom comes back. "Hannah loves animals."

"Most kids do."

"But she really does. She wants to be a . . . what's that you call it, a herp—"

"Herpetologist, Mom," Hannah says. She turns to me. "You're lucky. I wish I could work here."

"Maybe one day you will."

"Come, Hannah." The mom takes the girl's hand and I watch her walk away, crocodile tucked under her arm. I think about Joe and wonder what he will do with his extraordinary life.

When all the lizards are fed, I come back to Berry. She makes her way to the cage door, struggling to move in a straight line. Somehow she is correcting for the half circle her body makes when she tries to go forward. I ease my hands under her belly and lift, so she can stand up. "I've seen a wild blue female," I tell her. "You're going to be out there, too, basking on a great rock and turning blue as can be, and then one day you'll dig your nest."

I hear tires on gravel and watch a minibus pull into the parking area. Music coming from it gets loud as the doors slide open. People and bags pile out in a riot of laughter and a language I don't know.


For the next few days, mornings at the Mess smell like Christmas brunch back home. Pancakes, coffee, bacon, eggs fried in butter. There's no end to the laughter. Even though I can't understand what they're saying, I laugh too. And when the guy who's always cooking says, "Hello!" and hands me a plate of eggs and bacon, I shake my head and say, "No, thank you," thinking that for once I'd like to eat what's being offered. I point to myself. "Vegan."

He's not the least bit offended—he just gives the plate to the next girl. I get the granola and mix up a packet of soy milk and sit down at the table. Each of them says, "Good morning," and their faces are so friendly. No one cares what I'm eating or not eating, and I'm smiling right back and nodding my head and saying, "I like your shirt," to the guy with the lizard on the front. He doesn't understand until I point. "The lizard."

"Ah," he says, nodding. "Anegada iguana. *Pinguis.*"

I look closer and read the caption: ANEGADA IGUANA SURVEY TEAM, 2003, *Cyclura pinguis.* All of these people are wearing shirts with different reptiles on the front, or back. One says EXPLORE UTILA and has another kind of lizard on it.

Sandy walks in and there's a chorus of good-mornings. She gets herself coffee and sits down next to me. "You getting to know everyone?"

"It would help if I could speak the language."

"Yeah, I know. These guys are amazing."

With that, the volunteers get up to wash dishes and put away food. They fill water bottles from the cooler and go out the door.

"I saw one guy's shirt that said Anegada?"

"Their club is divided into groups that work with reptiles around the world. This group focuses on iguanas here in the West Indies. The Anegada iguana is almost as endangered as the blue."

"Same problems?"

"Sure, habitat loss, feral dogs. Also, there are goats loose on the island, eating the wild forage, and the iguanas go hungry. It's a mess. But folks are working on it, doing what they can. Got the captive breeding pens, and so on."

"I had no idea."

"How would you? It's not like they put this stuff on TV. Tell you what, there's no better time to go into field-work. The need is endless. The only drawback is, the pay sucks."

Early the next morning the birds singing in the gumbo-limbo tree are joined by banging hammers and a whining saw. The Reptile Club, building head-start cages. Walking to the Mess I catch the scent of Meg's strong coffee and I hurry up the steps. Sandy comes out on the porch to cut bananas. "Hey, we're just about to eat."

I'm surprised to see Josh at the table, studying papers, and Tom at the stove with a spatula, lifting eggs from the skillet while Meg holds the plates. "Morning," she says.

"Eat up," Tom tells me. "Big day ahead. You're going into new territory."

Suddenly I'm wide awake. I pour coffee and get the granola and bring my bowl to the table.

Tom says, "Some birdwatchers saw an iguana up by the northern zone. They said it didn't have beads. Of course, we can't be sure about that, but they did have binoculars. So you're going to hike in and cut a trail north."

In Tom's office, he touches a spot on the map. "Here's base camp, and here's the northern zone. And here," he says, tapping a patch that's all green, "is where they saw him. Her. Whatever. I need to know if females are traveling north."

"Why?"

"Because if they don't find nesting sites in the reserve, they might go looking by the coast." He points to a photo of the Salina, taken as if the photographer stood on a ladder. "That's the northern coast. What do you see beyond the forest?"

"A beach. Some buildings."

"And?"

"A road." My stomach clenches.

Tom gives me a camera and a clipboard with a legal pad. "You're going to take pictures. I need to know about vegetation, karst formations, oxisol. Things that make habitat iguana-friendly, where they are, and how much."

Meg puts her hand on my shoulder. "It's already getting hot out there."

I go put on my khakis and Meg's boots, and hurry back to help pack lunch. We get in the truck and Meg drives while Josh studies a map. I sit with the clipboard on my lap, figuring out a sort of key for myself so I can do diagrams quickly. I settle on X's for edible vegetation, diagonal lines to show the shape of karst outcroppings, and a single line to delineate oxisol patches, with an inch being ten paces.

Meg parks the truck at the entry to the Salina. We carry backpacks loaded with tracking and tagging equipment, plus water bottles and lunch, and make our way to base camp, where Josh picks up a trap. "Just in case," he says. Meg straps it onto the backpack. When we reach the end of the trail Josh pulls out the machete and starts hacking through the bush. Meg follows, stepping on cut branches, and I have my clipboard ready.

Josh says, "On the left, yellow-root."

It's a tangled mass of vines and leaves, and I snap a photo, then make a bunch of X's in a long, oval-shaped patch.

The racket we're making while cutting through the bush makes it hard to hear the birds and the rustling of leaves as small lizards scurry out of our way. Josh pauses now and then to point out patches of vegetation, and I take pictures and make X's on my diagram. We pass a huge outcropping of karst that looks very iguana-friendly. He looks over his shoulder and I say, "Got it."

The sun is right overhead and we're sweating through our shirts when Josh says, "There's a clearing to the right."

We take off backpacks and make a spot in the shade of a tree and eat our sandwiches. Not far off a flock of birds starts calling and chattering. "They sound like parrots," I say.

"They are," Josh says. "Grand Cayman parrots. Lets us know we're near the thick of the forest."

Meg looks at her GPS. "We're actually not far from where the birdwatchers saw the iguana."

"Then we should get going," Josh says, finishing his sandwich. "What time have you got?"

"Quiet," I say, putting my finger to my lips. They stop crumpling sandwich wrappers. A rustling. They hear it too. Getting closer, and then we see her. Big, like Sara. No beads—wild. She walks that dinosaur walk right through the clearing as if we aren't even there, and we look at each other, wide-eyed, unable to move. She tilts her head, and I can see that her eyes are on Meg's. Then her back drops and she trots the rest of the way into the bush.

We exhale. I turn to a blank page and write everything down as fast as I can. Josh baits the trap with banana.

Meg looks at her watch. "It's around two, so two-thirty, I come back."

We pack up and start cutting and hacking our way north, and I'm thinking, *No way are we going to catch a wild iguana, with all the noise.* Soon Meg says, "Time," and she walks back to check the trap while Josh keeps hacking into the bush. I'm making a patch of X's for more yellow-root when the cell beeps and Josh stops. "That's our signal."

With the trail cut it's easy going, and when we reach the clearing Meg is sitting near the trap with a palm frond over it for shade. "Check him out," she says, lifting it.

"Him?" Josh says.

He's nearly the size of Digger, a stony shade of gray. When Josh takes him out of the trap his jaws are open and he's whipping his tail and thrashing side to side. His eyes are so afraid it makes me sick in my stomach and I just want to let him go, but I hold him while Meg and Josh do their work.

The beads we're tagging him with are Orange-Red-

Green. "Dot Org," Meg says. I cringe when she puts the wire through his crest. He flinches. She puts three more beads on the other side and then flattens the tip with pliers. Josh puts in the PIT tag with a click. Last, Meg fits ORG with a radio transmitter. It's a twenty-minute ordeal.

Finally I get to release him. I think he's going to burst out of my hands, but he's gone limp, so I set him down on a palm frond and step back. He blinks and brings up his arms, slowly coming to all fours. He tilts his head and our eyes meet. His widen, showing red, and then he puffs up and runs into the bush so fast I put my hand to my chest.

The next morning I'm walking to the Mess, wondering if Tom has looked at my notes, when I see the cat with something blue. I run, yelling, "Drop it!" but the cat disappears, taking the blue something with her.

My heart pounding, I go after her, but the bush is thick and I lose sight. I hold still to listen for where she might be and there's a sick feeling in my guts. I follow what might be a path, pushing branches out of my way, and I find the bit of blue near a downed tree. A lizard, though not an iguana. It's awful. The cat ate the lizard's top half. Just his blue legs and tail are left.

I hear a sound inside the fallen tree. Crouching, I see pairs of shiny eyes and little triangle ears. I count four kittens, one black like mom, all with fur sticking straight out. There's hissing and spitting when I reach for them, and three retreat inside the log, but I catch the black one by the scruff. He doesn't fight; he's trembling, and I can't bear it. I hold the kitten against me and shelter him with my hands. He has fleas. I scan the bush for the mom and think of the half-eaten lizard that could have been a baby iguana, and his death would have been my fault. I put the kitten back with his siblings and walk to the Mess.

There are cages in the shed and a Havahart trap that looks like it's never been used. "Let's bait it," I say.

"You'll never catch that cat," Tom says. He's got the .22.

"We have to try."

"Feel free."

"We don't have to be cruel."

"I'm not being. You need to understand that cats don't belong here."

Sandy carries a cage for the kittens and I've got the trap. Tom goes into the bush. I bait the trap with a piece of chicken and set it a little ways from the tree. Then I start to feel defeated, because I know Tom's right.

I focus on the kittens. Sandy catches the black one. That's what kitty gets for trusting a human. I hold open the cage door and Sandy hesitates and smiles at the kitten. We look at each other. She puts him in and he starts to mew, a panicked sound. I go find a palm frond to cover the cage. Sandy reaches inside the log, and I hear a muffled little growl. When she puts the second kitten in with the black one, they huddle together, mewing in a pathetic chorus. She goes after another and pulls out a hissing ball of fur. She can't catch the fourth.

"Let me try." On my stomach I reach inside the log,

my shoulder coming against the jagged edge. My fingers brush fur and there's tapping, his little paw trying to bat me away. I could let him go, I could pull out and say, "No use." Instead I thrust my hand in, slamming my shoulder against wood, and my hand closes around the wriggling furry body. He snarls and spits and Sandy holds open the cage door and I put him in. They've stopped mewing and are just trying to hide in each other's fur.

"This is hard," she says.

"I hate it." The half-eaten lizard is still where the cat dropped it, and I go pick up the remains and lay them under a thatch palm.

Sandy is sitting cross-legged. "Barely broke the skin," she says, turning her hand over.

I look at my hand. There's a *crack!* and then another. It's familiar—the first shot brings the deer down, but sometimes another is needed.

Soon we hear Tom making his way through the bush. He's sweaty and his face is set. He gives Sandy the .22 and picks up the cage. "You two get going on the feeding."

Sandy puts the gun in Tom's office while I get out the sacks of food. I hear tires on gravel, leaving the parking area, heading for the pound.


It's Sunday and we're in the Jeep on our way to the beach with the warm, salty wind in our hair. I shut my eyes and breathe it in. "We're getting close."

"Less than a mile," Sandy says. I see a few palm trees

ahead, the big ones with coconuts. Meg starts putting on sunscreen. "The tide will be coming in."

The road takes a turn to the right, but we go left down a narrow one that's sandy with patches of weathered rock and stubby weeds growing up the middle. Sea grape branches scrape the sides of the Jeep, and then suddenly we're through. A white-sand beach spreads out before us, and beyond is the sea, brilliant blue and sparkling.

Meg shields her eyes. "Hardly any wind. Bet the guys do all right."

Josh went fishing with Tom and Willy, and we're meeting later for the birthday party for Timothy's grandmother, Mimi. We get our towels and head for the water. My feet sink in the dry sand, and it makes me think of dreams where if I try to run I just go slower. Near the high-tide line the beach firms up, and we leave our towels there. The water's barely cool, and my shoulders relax as I feel it rising up my legs.

"Perfect," Meg says, diving in. Sandy and I go all the way under, and then we float on our backs. I taste the salt. "I've never been in the ocean."

"No way!" Sandy says.

"It's amazing, I don't have to struggle to float."

"That's the salt water."

"It's bliss," Meg says.

I tilt my head back and my ears fill so that all I can hear is the ocean and my heart beating. The way the sky comes down to meet the sea around me, it's like I'm floating high above the earth. I look into a blue that goes on and on and I feel my ribs expand as I draw in air, and somehow

I know that things will be good. There's motion in the water close by. Holding my breath, I go under, but everything's blurry. I can just make out a few silver lines at the surface, moving away. It occurs to me that my eyes are open in salt water and it doesn't burn like I thought it would. I go up for air. "I saw a fish. Long and skinny."

Sandy comes to her feet. "Needlefish," she says, adjusting her bikini ties.

Meg ducks under and stands up, wet hair flat against her head, like mine. Sandy's is too curly to lie flat.

"Clarice, you're as dark as Meg now."

"Am I?"

I hold up my arm and Meg does too, so they're touching. "Even our scabs match," she says.

"I bet the beaches in California are nice," I say.

"Yes," Meg says. "But we hardly ever go. Too busy with work."

"Wish I was busy with work."

"You are."

"But it's going to end when I leave."

"So come back," Sandy says.

"I can't just come every summer, with no real plan."

"Then you need a plan."

I cup my hands in the water and make little waves that crash into each other. "College."

"Probably," Meg says.

"It always comes back to that."

"It gives you options," Sandy says. "Me, I'll never be a field biologist—"

"Never say never," Meg says.

"Whatever. I'm totally happy with what I do. But I'll be glad to have a degree, in case I decide to teach or something."

"My friend Polly's moving to New York City. She's going to be an actress. She'll do it, I know she will."

"Awesome. When she's rich and famous, she can make a big donation."

Back at BIRP we shower and get ready for dinner. I'm about to put on my kitty earrings, but then I look at the two silver faces in my hand, and I put on the dangly ones instead. They go better with my dress, which is also long and feels soft and loose around my legs as I'm walking to the Mess.

It's funny to see us in something besides khakis and iguana T-shirts. Sandy's got on a dress that's white and clingy, and Meg's is sort of a sage green and goes just past her knees. Around her ankle she's wearing a thin gold chain that looks nice above the delicate strap of her sandal. I'm wearing my Tevas, leather-free, and so *not* delicate.

"I like your earrings," she says.

"Thanks." I touch the loops of glass beads. "I hardly ever wear them."

Riding in the Jeep I run my hands through my hair, letting the wind dry it. I can't tell how far we've gone because Sandy's driving slowly, but soon she puts on the turn signal and we drive into a tropical version of suburbia. We pull up to a tall white fence draped with a blanket of bright pink flowers, and she makes a right into a short driveway. For a second it's like I'm back home, with the pickup trucks and fishing poles and garage stuff, only there aren't any snow shovels or skis. Josh, Timothy, and Tom are holding Caybrews and standing around a big cooler. I see the tip of a fish tail sticking up.

"Miss me?" Josh says, giving Meg a kiss.

I keep back from the cooler, but Sandy looks in. "Nice. Who got the yellowtail?"

"Who do you think?" Tom says. It's the first time I've seen him smile.

The front door opens and a big man who must be Timothy's dad comes out. "Meg! Sandra! How lovely to see you," he says, putting an arm around each for a hug. Then he takes my hand in both of his. "Clarice."

"My father, William," Timothy says.

"Please call me Willy."

"Willy," I say. "Thank you for having me to dinner."

"It is my pleasure. I hope everyone is hungry!"

"Starving," Sandy says.

"Mimi is in the garden and there are cold drinks waiting."

We go through the house and out French doors into a tropical garden. Terracotta pots are everywhere, with plants and flowers spilling from them. In the center, overgrown with more of the pink flowers, stands a pergola. To one side a table is set with glasses and linens, and beyond is a small building like a cottage.

A woman with wild white hair steps out and says, "Hello! Welcome to the garden." Her wrinkly skin is darker than Timothy's, and she's wearing a Hawaiian shirt and baggy shorts down to her knees. This must be Mimi.

"Happy birthday!" Sandy says. She and Meg give Mimi hugs.

"Happy birthday," I say, putting out my hand.

She gives it a good squeeze. "I'm delighted that you came."

"If my mom could see your garden, she'd move here."

"I came down when Timothy was born and I'll never go back."

"That's back to Minnesota," Sandy says. "Can you picture her in a coat and snow boots?" A hummingbird whizzes by and hovers around the pink flowers.

"Mimi, what are those?" I ask.

"Bougainvillea," she says, leading us to the pergola. Under the ceiling of vines and blossoms is a swing made of skinny logs, like the one we have on the porch back home.

Sandy eases herself into the seat and starts rocking it with her foot. "Finish the tour without me, I'm going to drift in paradise."

Meg and I follow Mimi out the other side, between raised beds. One is covered with gauze, protecting lettuces and herbs from the sun, and the other has tomato vines heavy with fruit growing up through round cages.

"Look how my tomatoes are coming on!" Mimi says. "It is next to impossible to grow a good tomato down here. The soil is poor, and there's so little of it. But I mix a fine compost with seaweed Tim brings me from the beach." She puts her hands in the loose pockets of her shorts and walks on toward a tree with fruit hanging like green Christmas bulbs. "Now, my oranges are another story. They do just fine with only a little help." Mimi pats the slender trunk. "This is a calamondin orange. The fruit is sour and full of seeds, but it makes the finest marmalade there is. And I'm sorry they won't be ready until November."

Meg says, "The avocados look ready."

"Yes, we'll have some with dinner."

When we get near the avocado tree a lizard with blue legs and tail scurries up the trunk and stops just out of reach.

"We had to collect some kittens," I say.

"Oh?"

"I saw a cat behind the Mess. I didn't know, and I fed her. Then I saw the kittens. They went to the pound and Tom shot her."

"He had to."

"I know."

The lizard pushes out his blue dewlap. Sunlight comes through and I think it looks like the wing of a fairy. "Back home we have these newts. Amphibians, only this big." I hold my hands apart three inches. "They're bright orange, with tiny spots. I had never seen a lizard until I came here. It's like seeing creatures from another world, or a different time, a million years ago. Or maybe from the future."

"Maybe the lizards will get the earth back." It's Timothy. "What do you think, Grandma?"

"I think it would be something to see."

"Let's eat," Timothy says.

At the table, Willy pours white wine and I accept a glass. Willy lifts his. "Happy birthday, Mimi," he says, and in a chorus of birthday cheers we clink glasses all around. The wine is cool and almost sweet. Tom, next to me, reaches over and pats the place on my arm where the lizard scabs are. "Those suit you," he says.

I can't keep from smiling. Timothy sees and my face warms. He raises his glass. "To good friends," he says. "And food from the garden and sea." Again we clink glasses and then we start passing dishes. The lobster is cut up in a salad, with green onions and lemon and what looks like a touch of mayonnaise. I'm grateful not to see the body and legs. Peas and rice, Willy says, is a traditional island dish that goes with just about every dinner. And then there are johnnycakes, another island staple. It's like a cross between corn bread and white cake, shaped into biscuits that are pan-fried. I let myself eat one, even though it's got to be made with butter.

I look at the late-afternoon light turning a patch of orange flowers to gold. There's the quiet that happens when hungry people start in on a good meal. I've never tasted avocado so sweet and buttery, and I've never seen it served like this, on a bed of yellow hibiscus petals and red lettuce. Tasting the flowers, I think of Billy. I love it that I'm eating lizard food.

Willy asks, "Are you getting enough to eat?"

"Yes, everything is delicious."

"To the cooks," Tom says, raising his glass. "How's Mom, Timothy?"

"Very well, we had a good visit. Ithaca is beautiful this time of year."

Mimi leans in my direction. "My daughter is happy to be away during summer. But I love the heat."

Willy says, "The Northeast is green, with grass everywhere, and the trees are tall and lush. I was there once, years ago."

"Back home in Pennsylvania, the day lilies are blooming. And by now my mom's sunflowers are tall as me."

"My goodness," Willy says. "I would very much love to see them. You must miss your family."

"Especially my brother, Joe. He shows me how to see animals and bugs."

Sandy's eyebrows go up. "And you say you're not a biologist."

"Not the kind that could get a real job."

"Willy runs a charter boat for fishing and sightseeing. He knows every animal on land or in the sea, right, Willy?"

Willy smiles. "I do okay." Then he whispers, "I didn't finish college."

Sandy nudges him. "Go ahead, tell Clarice how you and Lucinda met."

"I saw a boat hit a sea turtle. He was badly wounded by the propeller. There was blood and soon the sharks would have him. So I pulled him on board. He must have been three hundred pounds! I took him to the animal hospital. When I first saw her, she was wearing her white doctor's coat, and those soft black curls could not be contained by the barrette. My hands were dirty with dried blood, but she took one and held it while she thanked me for bringing the turtle. When she smiled I thought I would fall down! Well, I came back to see how the turtle was doing. He made it, you know? In one week they moved him to a pen at the docks and then he went free. And I showed Lucinda the islands."

Sandy brings her hand to her chest. "I love that story."

"The turtle must have been amazing," Meg says.

"Yeah, I wish I'd been there to see him swim away," I add.

Timothy says, "I've got a photo, taken just before he was released."

"Who would like coffee?" Willy asks. Sandy helps clear dishes while Meg and I follow Timothy. In his room there's a map that's mostly blue and so big it covers the wall. The Cayman Islands are little spots in the midst of an immense sea, marked with all these lines and numbers that must be about depth and current and underwater topography. The desk and shelves are stacked with textbooks—*Organic Chemistry, Invertebrate Zoology, Oceanography.* Above the computer are shelves crowded with all kinds of seashells. There's no order to their arrangement, yet they are placed as though each one is held and studied and carefully put back.

"What's that one on top? It looks like an ostrich egg."

"The test of a sea urchin." He takes down the shell and puts it in my hand. It's weightless and there are tiny holes and knobs all over.

"Echinodermata," he says.

"What?"

"Spiny skin. It's the phylum with starfishes and sea urchins. The spines fit on the knobs, and the little holes are where the tube feet came out." He finds a penlight on the desk. "Hold it over the light."

I do, and the whole thing glows like the moon. The pinpoints of light and knobs are in the shape of a starfish resting on top, with the tips of his feet meeting underneath. I run my finger across the fragile shell and wonder about the animal who lived inside.

"This is the biggest conch I've ever seen," Meg says, picking up a shell the size of a cantaloupe and turning it in her hand. "No hole."

"I like to think he died of old age."

"How could you know?" I ask.

"Most conchs have a hole where they whack the crown with a knife and cut the muscle."

I shudder. "Yuck, that's awful."

Meg puts the shell back in its place. "Conch was a major source of protein in the islands."

"My dad says when he was a boy, they hung it on a clothesline and made jerky. They called it hurricane beef, because it kept everyone fed when boats couldn't go out."

"Still," I say, crossing my arms.

"Whoa," Meg says, looking at a photo on the dresser. "Check out the size of the turtle."

"He's the reason I'm here," Timothy says. "And that's my mom," he tells me.

"She's beautiful," I say. Her dark curls spill out of the

barrette, just as Willy said. She's kneeling beside the turtle, resting a hand on his shell. I'm fascinated by the enormous flipper that faces the camera. It's so different from a snapping turtle's foot, yet both species are aquatic. Then I think how snappers walk on land, between bodies of water. Across roads.

"He may still be out there," Timothy says.

"You don't want to be a veterinarian?"

He shakes his head. "I need to be out on the water, or in it."

"So you've been diving a long time."

"Since I was nine."

"What is that like, to breathe under water and swim with the fish? I've only seen it on TV."

"If you want to, we could go snorkeling."

"Really? That would be awesome."

"I'm helping Dad on the boat this Saturday, but the one after is free. We could all go, I've got enough gear."

"Thanks," Meg says, "but that will be a tough weekend. It's crunch time and there's a lot to wrap up before we leave."

"Who's got matches?" Sandy is in the doorway holding a cake with candles on top. "One for each decade, plus a half for the five."

After dessert we say our thanks and goodbyes to Willy and Mimi. "Don't forget," Timothy says. "Two weeks, we have a date."

"Thirteen days," I say.

Meg, Josh, and I get in the BIRP truck and follow

Sandy's Jeep and Tom's little pickup to the end of the street, and then Josh beeps the horn as we go our separate ways.

Stars are out and the air is warm. Back home, it's the same, plus there's the moist, green smell of late summer. But I like this salty ocean smell. Until now I haven't even thought about the plane ticket and passport waiting at the bottom of the drawer in my little room.

"You're awfully quiet," Meg says.

"I feel like I just got here and I'm—I need more time. To figure things out."

Josh says, "You've got another four weeks, right? A lot can happen between now and then."


Monday morning Sandy gets called in to work the lunch shift, and the Reptile Club is packing up to leave. Meg and Josh are out in the Salina and I lose myself with the iguanas. It's not so unlike being at the SPCA, the way I'd be with the animals and my own thoughts. I wonder why I don't just get a full-time job at an animal shelter.

At the end of the row I find Berry on her back, struggling. There's a piece of plywood on top of the cage. I open the door, ease my hand under, and turn her over. She blinks and licks her lips. Her breath is labored. Leaning against my hand helps her relax. I rest my arm on the doorframe so we can stay like that a while. I watch the heaving of her ribs slow down, her breathing return to normal, almost. Hearing footsteps, I turn to see Tom.

"Checking on your friend?"

"She was on her back."

"I found her like that the day before yesterday and put up the plywood for extra shade. She can't be on her back in the sun for long, or she'll cook."

I put my hand on Berry as if to protect her. "I don't understand. I thought she was getting better."

"She is growing in spite of the injury, like a sapling pushing against a fallen tree. You've noticed how she's more active, which is how she gets herself tipped over. And she's losing her baby face."

I pull a hibiscus flower from my pocket and stroke her shoulder with my thumb while she eats. Tom watches, hands on his waist in that time-to-get-to-work way. "The sooner we know if she can recover, the better."

"What if she can't?"

"What kind of life would you want for her?"

I don't answer, I just start rubbing Berry's back, getting her ready to stretch.

"Keep at it, Clarice," he says, and walks away.

I cradle Berry in my hands and realize that Tom is right about the changes. When she blinks I see the red sclera better. Her nose isn't so stubby and her jaw and neck are longer. She props herself up, pushing against my thumb with her right hand. I see the muscles in her arm working to steady her body. Brave girl.

My eyes sting and I lift her to my face and rest my cheek on her shoulder. She lets me, doesn't tense up, and that makes me feel better. Maybe I'll just have to care for her always. I imagine her back home, resting on my pillow with a heat lamp fixed to the bedpost. I could grow food for her—find leaves and flowers for her to eat. Joe would be thrilled. She moves her foot, and I snap out of my fantasy and get back to work on her crooked spine.

When we're done I am tempted to take her with me, maybe set her up in my room for the night. My hands are like a brace and I don't want to take them away. But finally I set Berry down in the cage, figuring she should be near her siblings, sleeping under the stars, as though it will keep her on the path to a life like GRG's out in the Salina.

I pick more hibiscus flowers and take them to Billy. He is sprawled on the sand, warming his belly in late-afternoon sun, when he sees me holding a flower. He comes to me quicker than before and takes it. I give him more. "Billy," I say, "your little cousin Berry is having a rough time."

As if trying to understand he looks into my eyes in that way that unsettles and moves me. Somehow I get that it's not my words he's curious about, it's me, my intent, my place in the scheme of things. I want to touch him; I want him to know me. Billy's head is bigger than my fist, and I think of the scars Sandy and Meg have. He waits. I give him the last flower. "Would you let me pet you?"

I take a breath and put one leg over the wall and then the other. I'm standing right in front of him, and he's not running away. I ask again, "Can I pet you?" and then I bend my knees and lower myself slowly. We're eye to eye, he's just an arm's length away, and I feel my heart beating. His dewlap is out a little, and Sandy told me that means an iguana's wary. Another deep breath and I reach out with my hand, low and to the side, so he can see. With the backs of my fingers I stroke his chin and then his jowls. His dewlap stays out, but he shuts his eyes.

"I think you like that," I say, charged by the contact and trying to stay calm. Not wanting to push my luck, I slowly pull back my hand. After a moment, I stand up, keeping all my moves slow, and I walk over to Billy's rock and sit down, hoping that's okay with him.

Billy's watching me the whole way, but he has pulled in his dewlap. I look around the pen and see Deborah near the back wall in a patch of sunshine, keeping an eye on me. After a long moment Billy walks toward me, then stops and sits just a few feet away. I look at his blue head and shoulders, the tall crest of spines down his back and on part of his tail. He must know the flowers are gone, but still he comes toward me and flicks out his tongue on my sneakers, the way a garter snake does. And then he tries to climb my leg, but his claws can't get a grip, so I reach down and help him into my lap. My heart is beating wildly and I can't quite believe I just did that. His strong-looking jaws are not far from my face. I straighten my back to give us both a few more inches of distance.

Billy sits on my thigh with my left hand supporting his legs. He's heavy and his belly is warm from the sun. He tilts his head and peers into my eyes. This close, it's even more intense, and I have to remind myself to breathe. Billy's look is like a dog's when he's trying to figure me out—and yet it's also very different. With their eyes, shelter dogs beg to be petted and talked to and taken home. Billy doesn't want me to take him anywhere, and though he may like being petted, I don't believe it's what he's seeking. He doesn't need any food right now, either—there's still some in his dish. What he wants, it's something I can't know. I can just hear Mr. Bloom: *Small, reptilian brain.* Scientists have cut up enough lizards to know that. A shudder goes through me at the thought of anything happening to Billy. I touch his scaly, warm back and the crest of spines. They are tougher than Berry's. I want to gather him up and hold on, but I don't want to scare him, and so we just sit like that for a while, until he gets restless and climbs down and walks his dinosaur walk to see his mate.

That night I do a pretty good job of sketching Billy's face. The scaly lips, nostrils, and eyes I've drawn make him look like Billy and not Digger or Macho. I was so enchanted sitting with him that I'm amazed my head was functioning enough to record such details. I wish I could figure out my attraction. He *is* like a dinosaur, alive here and now, so animated and yet so *other.* His eyes seem to ask, *Who are you?* I remember Joe when he was two and I was eleven. I toted him around on my hip the way Sandy holds Digger. I loved the feel of his arms and legs clinging to me, and I loved feeling like I was protecting him. I'd imagine holding on tight and fighting off a wild dog. If a wild dog—or a person—tried to hurt Billy, I'd do the same: I'd gather him to me and draw my sword with a *shing!*

Sun-up to sundown my days are heavenly, whether I'm in the Salina with Meg and Josh or feeding the iguanas. Sandy and I take flowers from the hibiscus hedge, half sneaking, giggling, trying not to strip the bushes completely. While Sandy is with Digger I sit on Billy's rock and feed him flowers one at a time. Then I visit some of the others. There's Eldemire, who looks like a craggy old dragon, with his long, floppy crest of spines and underbite that shows a few teeth. But he is totally gentle and shuts his eyes tight when I give him a back scratch. Then there's Pedro, who flushes so blue when I pet him that he almost doesn't look real. And gorgeous Yellow, who patrols his territory constantly and seems too preoccupied with his own exquisiteness to be bothered with affection from humans. It just makes him all the more adorable.

On Salina days, when we get back to the Mess we peel off our boots and get cold drinks that taste incredibly good after having warm water out of plastic bottles all day. We sit on the porch and press the cold, wet glasses against our cheeks. Macho visits and we take turns giving him pieces of banana. There's talk of dinner and I get up to work with Berry and check in with Billy.

But on Thursday Tom is waiting on the porch. He's having a beer already. "Clarice," he says, "let's talk."

My heart pounds in my chest. Images flip through my head—something I did, a cage door not shut. "Who got hurt?"

Tom looks at me and I start freaking out inside.

"Did someone call from home?"

"Nothing like that. Let's go inside."

Tom holds open the screen door for me. He drops his empty bottle in the bin and goes to the fridge, takes out two bottles, opens them, and hands me one. "Thanks," I say, even though I don't want a beer. I'm trembling; I grip the bottle for something to hold on to.

We go inside the office. It couldn't be a bad screw-up, because he doesn't shut the door. He sits in his chair and I perch on the edge of another.

"Blueberry is in pain," he says.

"Then I'll stay here and be with her. Meg and Josh don't need me."

"No, there's nothing you or any of us can do."

"But she's getting better, she's growing."

"Yes, but it's not going well. The spine is not straightening. Her organs are being compressed."

"Then she needs surgery."

Tom shakes his head. "Won't work."

"Why not?"

"Surgery on the spine is too complicated. Even if it could work, the recovery would be drawn out and painful. You don't want her to endure that."

"How do you know all this?"

"Took her to see the vet. This morning I found her on her back again. But this time she wasn't just struggling, she was gasping. The doctor shot her up with painkiller. Should keep her comfortable for twenty-four hours. We have an appointment in the morning."

Tom and I are looking at each other. My throat is tight. Tom takes a long drink from his beer, and so do I.

. . .

In the morning Meg gives me a hug before she and Josh leave for the Salina. Tom drives while I hold Berry curled against my chest. She's calm, no doubt from the drugs. She blinks more slowly than usual, like a sleepy baby. Watching her makes my eyes fill, so I watch the road ahead.

I am grateful that the doctor doesn't try to take Blueberry away from me. He gives her an injection in her leg and says, "This will ease her into a deep sleep. Then we'll give the phenobarbital."

I feel Blueberry's body relaxing, her legs getting heavier and going limp. Her head leans to one side and her eyes stay shut, but she's still breathing. She lets go of her bowels. The doctor gives me a towel. Then he fills a huge syringe from a bottle. *It's not too late,* I think. *I can stop it. Blueberry will wake up in a couple of hours and we'll figure out what to do, we'll make a plan.* Instead I hold still, hold Blueberry close, and then I can't stop, tears roll down. Tom takes the soiled towel and gives me some Kleenex. The doctor gives the injection and Blueberry doesn't flinch. She's in dreamland.

It takes a long time for Blueberry's heart to stop. The doctor checks every ten minutes for an hour. I hold her foot in my hand and look at the spots on her long toes. I've always felt that euthanasia was a good thing. End the suffering. I remember when this guy brought in a kitten that had been hit by a car and had a smashed pelvis. The crying was pitiful. As far as I was concerned, we couldn't put the kitten down fast enough. Somehow this is different.

After a while the doctor takes Blueberry from me and

wraps her in a towel and directs me to the sink to wash up. It's strange that I have a moment of relief, as if I am washing grief from my hands. It doesn't last, though. I can still feel Blueberry in my hands and I can still see her face. My eyes well up again.

I'm thinking about where to bury her when Tom says they want her body. "She's not a pet," he says. "Blueberry has the opportunity to help her species in her own way."

I wonder what can be learned from her bent little body.


When Tom pulls the truck in at the Mess, I see Timothy's red Ford parked. I wipe my eyes and run my fingers through my hair and thank Tom for letting me hold Berry while she died.

Sandy and Timothy are feeding the head-start iguanas. I walk out there and look in Berry's cage. I'd swear her siblings are unhappy. Sandy puts her arms around me. "We didn't feed Billy and Deborah."

Timothy gives me the bucket of food and I realize he's letting me be alone. But I say, "Want to help?"

"Go ahead," Sandy says. "I'll finish up here."

I put food in Billy and Deborah's dish and sit with Timothy on the pen wall. He doesn't say anything about Berry, which is good, because I don't want the waterworks to start again. After eating just a few bites, Billy comes to us.

"I've been giving him lots of treats. He lets me pet him now." I reach down and stroke his back and he flicks my sneaker with his tongue.

"He's curious about you."

"Yeah, it's one of the cool things I'm learning about these guys."

"When I go diving, the fish check me out. Some get very close and others watch from their hiding places in the coral. Maybe they see me as a predator, or maybe as food, but either way they're curious about me, for sure."

"People don't talk that way about animals back home. I mean, they don't think of them as being curious." I tuck the hair behind my ears. "What's strange to me is how kids in 4-H love their hogs and lambs and then sell them to be eaten."

"Well, I eat fish."

"I'm beginning to think it's different."

"How so?"

"The way you talk it's like you include yourself in the animal kingdom. Like Native Americans, the way they cared about buffalo and also ate them. They had reverence for life."

He smiles.

"Am I wrong?"

"Maybe just a bit romantic."

Billy turns, his body and tail making a complete circle, which he exits on a path to his mate. We watch the lizards finish their meal, and then Billy climbs his rock, looks over his territory, and settles himself. With half-shut eyes, he has an expression that says all's well in his world. Deborah finds the last leaf and turns from the dish. I watch her walk the dinosaur walk, her spine a fluid S, moving side to side with each step, long tail out behind. She goes to her favorite patch of sand and spreads her belly and limbs to soak up heat from the sun. Lucky girl. Whole, alive, her mate close by, her life ahead.

When Meg and Josh get back, we all climb into the BIRP truck and go to Johnny's. People are crowded around the bar, and the tables are full, but the waiter seats us right away. "Tom knows the manager," Sandy tells me.

Tom holds up his hand like he's going to high-five the waiter. "Five Caybrews. And a coconut juice for the young lady. Dinner's on me, folks."

When the drinks come, Tom pours some beer in a glass and passes it to me, then raises his bottle. "To Blueberry."

We clink glasses and the waiter takes our order. Tom starts talking to Sandy about landscaping in the pens, and Josh says something to Meg about a thesis. "Berry tried hard," I tell Timothy. "After I worked with her she always stood right up. You could see the muscles in her legs tremble with the effort." My eyes sting and it's hard to swallow. "I understand that we did the right thing. But still, with all our technology—I mean, if we can put a camera inside someone's joint and do all this microsurgery . . ."

"I'm sorry," he says. "It's very sad."

I have a sip of beer, and it goes right to my head. I wipe my eyes and let out a breath. "I'd still like to go tomorrow."

"Shall I pick you up after lunch?"

"Yes, please."

The food comes and Tom asks about the day. Meg says, "We tracked Dot Org circling back southwest and then north again. Clearly he's staying in the area where the female was."

Tom nods. "We need to tag that female and see if she's moving any farther north."

"So, what would drive her?" I ask.

"Drought, which affects edible plants. Competition for nest sites if the iguana population rises, which it will when we do the next release." Tom leans back in his chair and takes a swig of beer. "Clarice, your field notes are solid. That little code of lines and X's is simple and clear. You've given me a picture of those iguanas. How the female acted when she came into view, how Dot Org was after release."

"Thanks, but I don't see how that's helpful."

"The BIRP goal is not just about getting data, it's about building a relationship with the iguanas and their habitat."

"To educate the public as best we can," Sandy says. "People protect what they love."

*That's right.* And I realize I know what Tom's talking about, and how the BIRP plan works. It makes total sense to me—it's not just a bunch of baffling science stuff.

"Here's to each of you for making BIRP the success that it is." Tom raises his glass. "And to winning the race against extinction."

With that we clink bottles and glasses like it's New Year's Eve.


Timothy is driving just fast enough to keep air moving through the cab. The sky seems more blue and vast than ever. I see a turkey vulture circling overhead and wonder what they find to eat, since there's no roadkill. "I can imagine driving here."

"How do you mean?"

"I don't drive. Everyone goes too fast and animals get hit constantly."

"Pennsylvania is big. I can understand why people drive fast."

"Yeah, but it's not like they have to cross the state—they're mostly going to work or to the mall. Everyone's just in a hurry all the time."

"I suppose we take it a bit slower on the island. But on the north coast by the resorts, cars go very fast."

"Tom's concerned about iguanas crossing that road."

"Speaking of which . . ." he says, slowing way down. Moving more like a snake, the lizard is across and out of sight by the time we get there.

"Not a blue," I say, impressed that Timothy saw him first.

"An ameiva. Fairly common."

"They're fast. Not like frogs. I hit one, and that's when I stopped."

"You stopped the car."

"My dad's truck, yeah. And I quit learning to drive."

"Then what do you do?"

"Ride my bike."

"I guess it's one way to avoid hurting animals."

"Josh told me about this sect in India, the Jains? They're so against causing harm that they wear a piece of cloth over their mouths to keep from swallowing insects by accident."

"I could never be a part of it. I kill thousands of microscopic animals every time I dive."

"We're such a destructive species."

"Well, I can't argue with you about that."

A salty breeze moves through the cab and I breathe it in. "So different here, the smell of the sea. It's not musky, like in the States."

"The northeastern sea is rich in plankton. That's why whales go there to feed during the summer." Timothy shifts gears and we go down the narrow road between sea grape branches. Then we're through, and he stops the truck. A tall white bird walks at the edge of the water, his long neck making an S.

"He's hunting, the way herons do back home."

"An egret," Timothy says. "A close relative."

When we get out of the truck, the bird lifts off and goes up the beach before coming down to continue fishing. Timothy carries two mesh bags, one with fins, the other with masks and snorkels. Mine isn't heavy, just water bottles and towels and energy bars, but it's slow-going in the dry sand. Timothy's calf muscles flex—he's used to it. He reaches for my bag and puts the strap over his shoulder.

Where the sand is firm Timothy stops and puts down our stuff, and we spread our towels. He takes off his shirt and rolls it up. I look out across the ocean.

"You can see where the reef is," he says, pointing. "Where the brown patches are. It's built by hundreds of corals. Elkhorn and giant brain are the ones you'll see the most. You mustn't touch them, by the way."

"Are they dangerous?"

"You are to them. Tiny, fragile animals make coral. Just brushing against it kills entire colonies."

"Maybe we shouldn't go where the coral is."

"If you want to see fish and other animals, we have to." His voice is patient. Our eyes meet and he smiles. "Just be careful, that's all."

"Okay." I roll up my T-shirt and put it on the towel.

"Use plenty of sunblock on the backs of your arms and legs." He takes out the water bottles and digs a hole in the wet sand and buries them.

After we get our fins on, we walk backwards into the water until we're knee-deep, and then we turn to face each other. There is a froth of white where the edge of the ocean touches the sand, but otherwise the surface is glassy and the water is so clear I can read sea diver on the tops of my fins. Timothy has our masks, and from a small bottle he squeezes a drop of baby shampoo into each one. "To help keep the glass from fogging."

We clean our masks and Timothy is ready to put his on. "The snorkel goes here," he says, showing me where to push it up between the strap and the side of my face. "Forget you have a nose at all. Just breathe only through your snorkel."

I bite my lower lip and focus on what I'm doing, which is putting on my mask the way Timothy did, stretching the strap and trying to fit it over my head. Timothy looks through his mask to see how I'm doing, and I giggle. His upper lip is pulled by the edge of the mask, giving him a goofy grin.

"Come on," he says, "put yours on. I want to see how funny you look." He sounds like he has a cold, with the mask covering his nose.

"Okay, okay." I pull the strap down onto the back of my head and let the mask cover my eyes and nose. Timothy reaches up and gently pulls back a bit of my hair that's caught in the strap. As soon as the mask is on I feel it seal and stretch my upper lip.

Timothy grins. "That's better." He puts the snorkel in his mouth and motions toward the open water and then he's in.

I put in my snorkel and try to turn, which makes me fall over my fins, but it's okay, the ocean catches me. I float on my stomach and blow salt water out of the snorkel. The sound of breathing is like in winter, when I cup my hands and exhale to warm my fingers. I lift my head to check on the world above. The water's surface is a liquid mirror that divides my view. The top half is blue sky and sparkling water and Timothy's snorkel sticking up. The bottom half is the sea. I go into it and catch up with Timothy.

We are like birds flying in a world of sea creatures. I see a fish, half yellow, half purple, dart under a reddish brown sphere that has lines and channels in swirls all over and must be the brain coral Timothy talked about. Other fish swim around the coral, one with pink stripes and big eyes watching me, another that's pure yellow with a spot by his tail like a blue eye. I see one little fish that's black with neon-blue spots all over. The moment I look at one incredible fish, another comes into view. My eyes focus on a jellyfish right in front of my mask. He's the size of a grape, transparent, with white, hairlike things that outline his body like stripes on a watermelon. One end pulses, moving him through the water.

With the fins on I barely have to kick to move forward, and I let my arms go back along my sides the way the lizards do when they bask. Everywhere is life, color, motion. I have to remind myself to paddle or I start to drift. Timothy must know I'm in sensory overload—he stays close by, matching my awkward pace. Three fish the size of footballs, mottled red and green, move like submarines just above the ocean floor, and from out of nowhere a fourth joins them, and he is bright blue. They don't seem afraid of us and come closer, and I take a deep breath and my mask goes tight around my face. I shake my head in a panic, because I've confused myself about how to breathe. Timothy touches my arm and points up. We stop and tread water. I spit out my snorkel and gasp. He slips a finger under the edge of my mask and breaks the seal. Then he takes his snorkel out of his mouth. "You used your nose."

"Yeah, those fish!" I say, sounding like my head's still under water. "Timothy, I can't believe it—I've never seen anything like it. For real, I mean. I'm *in* it!"

He grins with his stretched-out lip and puts his snorkel back in and we go under. Nudging my arm, he points at a huge cluster of coral like a forest of extra-thick antlers.

In the midst I see a black-and-white-spotted snake and then I realize it's an eel. As we come closer, he pulls himself partway into the coral. His mouth opens and shuts, showing teeth that look sharp, but the movement is more like respiration than a warning.

Again Timothy nudges me. This time it's a lobster with long, spiky antennae. We paddle above him and I see that he has no big claws but lots of legs, and they're all in motion, so he's kind of dancing on tiptoes, watching us and keeping his back to his retreat in the coral. I sense a big shadow and look to my right. I remember not to use my nose when I catch my breath seeing the school of fish nearly upon us. There must be a thousand, each one the size of my hand, yellow with thin blue stripes. All at once they turn, their scales reflecting light, and they become a silver wave, moving away from us.

The floor of the reef between coral cities is a vast suburb, fuzzy with sand-colored weeds, and there are little holes like windows into rooms with movement inside, creatures I can't see completely. Tucked in here and there are black sea urchins, their spines in motion like rays of sun. A clump of the floor moves—a small crab wearing a coat of furry weeds. Every inch is alive. Even in the water around me, more tiny jellyfish float like glass orbs.

I feel Timothy take my hand. He points to a long, silver-gray object, and as we swim closer I realize that the object is coming closer to us and that it's a big fish. Timothy stops paddling and so do I. The fish is not a shark, so I am not really nervous, even though he is almost as long as I am. He's sort of hanging in the water, watching us with his big silver eye. The pupil is the size of a nickel and black as oil. His gills flap in slow motion and some of his teeth show, pointy and white. *Barracuda.* Dark stripes go down his sides, fading as they reach his silver-white belly. He seems to be getting closer. Timothy lets go of my hand and drops below the surface and moves toward the barracuda, bubbles coming out the end of his snorkel. The fish turns and in an instant he's a bit of silver in the distance. I blow air out my snorkel, unable to believe how fast he moved.

We haven't gone far when Timothy takes my hand again. Shapes are coming toward us—three creatures with triangular wings. They're like the manta rays I've seen on TV, but they are spotted on their backs and white underneath. We hang in the water like skydivers in free fall while they circle us, flying in slow motion with tails like thin lines streaming out behind. I see their eyes move as if they're studying us, though I can't make eye contact with them, possibly because of my mask. Suddenly they flap their wings and swim away in a burst of speed. Again I have to remind myself how to breathe under water.

Timothy taps his wrist where a watch would be and he points to land. I don't want it to end. But as we swim toward shore I feel how cold my hands and feet are.

We sit on our towels unwrapping energy bars. My goose bumps are melting and I lick salt from my lips. "Those weren't manta rays, but what were they?"

"Eagle rays."

"They *circled* us."

"Sometimes they leap from the water, like dolphins. People say they're shaking off remoras, but I say they're just happy."

"I wanted to communicate with them. I *felt* something."

"What would you say?"

"I'd thank them for coming so near." I push sand into a mound and think of Joe building huts for bugs. "When did you know you wanted to be a marine biologist?"

He laughs.

"What?"

"Mimi, rolling up those baggy shorts of hers. We'd walk in the tide pools, and she'd hold my hand when I lost my balance. She never tired of looking into crevices in the rocks and following little crabs. We discovered countless sea creatures. One time, two boys in masks and snorkels came out of the water with a big starfish. I said, 'Mimi! They have a starfish.' She took my hand. 'Look, a school of minnows, coming to us.' I couldn't leave it alone, though, and I kept looking back at the boys. They pulled off their gear and sat on the beach. The starfish lay in the sun and I knew that he was dying. I tugged on Mimi's hand until she let go and I went over there and said, 'Please put him back.' 'It's ours,' they said, 'go find your own.'"

"But you didn't want the starfish for yourself."

"I know." He puts his arms around his knees and looks out at the ocean. "So you think I'd be a good teacher?"

"Definitely. Is that what you want to do?"

"What I really want is to start a diving school. To train divers for conservation work."

"Bet you will." I pull my knees up to my chin and bury my toes in the sand. He loves the sea and the animals who live there, yet he eats some of them, and I want to be okay with that. Then I think about how people eat iguanas, too, and I see pictures of Billy being hurt and I cover my eyes.

"What is it?"

"Sorry. Awful things come into my head sometimes." I scoop sand and let it run through my fingers.

Timothy takes my hand. After a while he says, "Want to go out again?"

"Yes!"

He pulls me to my feet. We put on our flippers, pick up our masks and snorkels, and do our duck walk into the sea.

When we get back, a rain shower has passed and the air is clear, the lines of things crisp. The BIRP truck is out, and Sandy has gone to work. Macho basks on the porch step, his skin still wet and brilliant blue. He's in a good mood.

Timothy brings my bag and sets it down on the porch. I would've forgotten about it. I drape my wet towel over a chair. "Thank you. That was so amazing."

"It was great fun. Maybe we can go again soon."

"I'd love that." My hair hangs in damp, salty strings, and I tuck it behind my ears.

He gives me a hug. "Enjoy the evening. You too, Macho." He gets in his truck, waves, and drives out the gate. I look at the two lizard silhouettes on the bars, facing each other. Dragons guarding the entry.

The birds are quiet, and there's no breeze to rattle palm fronds. I break off a banana and give it to Macho. He eats it in three bites instead of two. I take another and walk to the hibiscus hedge. The sun makes the raindrops like crystal beads and I hold up a flower and let a few fall in my mouth. They are sweet and I try not to shake them off as I pick.

When I get closer to his pen, Billy sees and comes to the wall in his high-up dinosaur stride. He is a mellow shade of blue. I climb in and kneel and spread the fruit and flowers on the ground. "All for you," I tell him. "No more sharing with Berry." I stroke his scaly back and watch the muscles in his neck and jaw move as he eats. He's so big, so alive. I look at his feet, his toes with sharp, curved claws, his spiky crest and red eyes. It doesn't matter that I've been working with these lizards for weeks—I'm still in awe, like a little kid seeing a frog for the first time. Maybe this is how Joe feels each time he sits with his bug friends.

That night I don't wash away the sea salt. I like the faint mineral smell and the way the salt makes my hair feel thick and almost wavy, and I think of Polly and wonder if she's moved into an apartment and found a job. I put on my extra-large BIRP shirt and lie down on the bed. Drawing in my journal is impossible, I'm too tired, and yet I can't be still. I think about the eagle rays and how I wanted so much to talk to them. It's like that with Billy and the others— Dot Org, Wiggly, GRG. And Berry. How I wish she could've known that I loved her. I wish I could tell the iguanas how happy they make me, just seeing them.

I hear a door shut—Meg and Josh, getting in late. Wrapping up their work, leaving Monday. I bet they stayed in the Salina till dusk, or maybe they ended up at the beach to see the sun go down. There's just enough light to make out two pairs of eyes on the ceiling right over me. My gecko guardians. I tell them that I love them.

The next thing I know, gray light is coming in the window. It's Sunday and I could shut my eyes and go back under water, with the rays. But I want to see my iguanas and people, so I splash water on my face and get dressed. In the gumbo-limbo tree, grackles make their whistling, musical calls and the air is cool, but not enough to give me goose bumps. The light is kind of hazy and makes me think of late August back home, when I wake up early like this, because there's a bit of summer left and I want to have every minute of it. A cup of coffee will be really nice. It's so early I bet mine will be the first pot. I'll make it strong, like Meg does.

I yawn and stretch my arms behind my back, and then I smile to myself, because I've seen the iguanas do the same things. Up ahead I see a lizard. Macho. I rub my eyes. That's odd—he's lying on his side. He's not moving, but it is early and the air is cool, so he should be in his burrow. Then it hits me that it's not Macho, it's Eldemire, out of his pen, and there's another lizard beyond him. Something's not right and I'm running and I drop to my knees and vomit when I see a bloody raw patch where Eldemire's leg should be. My stomach surges, but I am able to start yelling for help, loud as I can. The other lizard is alive. Jessica. Eldemire is dead. His eyes are shut tight; his arm is in the air as if trying to push away what hurt him. I put my hands on him like that will help. Footsteps running behind me. "What's going on?" It's Meg. "Why is Jessica out?" She starts yelling, "Josh! Call Tom. Call the police!"

Meg doesn't wait, she runs inside the Mess. More footsteps running. Josh goes to Jessica. "Don't move her until Tom gets here." He takes off for the head-start cages.

I kneel beside Jessica. Dazed, eyes wide open, not meeting mine. I want to hold her and say, *It's going to be okay, whatever hurts, we'll fix it,* but I can't see where the hurt is and I don't know what to do. *Billy.* My heart pounding, I get up and run to his pen and jump over the wall. At the sight of spattered blood, I gag and spit up acid. "Billy, where are you?" Then I see him and I'm on my knees again. He is cut, his arm is opened up, and muscle shows purple-red. I feel myself wanting to heave again, but my stomach's empty and what comes over me is awareness that my help is needed now. Like Jessica, he's dazed and staring.

I put my hand out to him, unable to think of what to do. He looks at me, his red eye meeting mine, and then he shuts it, shutting out the world and me with it. I hear a siren finally, tires on gravel and the slam of car doors. I yell, "Billy's hurt!" and then I hear a terrible cry from Digger's pen. I go running and Sandy is on her knees, rocking Digger's limp body in her arms. His head hangs loose to one side.

Tom stays with Jessica, shading her from the sun. Josh comes running and says, "Sara is dead. And Yellow.

Matthias and Archie are injured. I can't find Pedro. None of the cages are damaged."

Tom's eyes are red and he wipes them.

"Billy's hurt too," I say.

"How bad?"

"His arm. Cut deep. I can't tell what else."

A white van pulls in, the veterinarian.

"Jessica first," Tom calls out.

The vet nods and gets out a small stretcher and they carry her inside. I stay with Meg to see what can be done for Sandy, who is still sobbing into Digger's body.

After tending to Jessica the vet sutures Billy's arm and says he's got a large bruised area on his back and that ribs may be broken. Matthias and Archie are also badly injured, with possible fractures and internal bleeding.


By afternoon, detectives, police, and reporters are asking questions and taking photos. Four bodies are lined up side by side. Sunken eyes, arms and legs limp, skin ashy gray. No blue, not happy. Dead.

The phone rings and rings. Tom goes back and forth between his desk and Jessica. She seems stable, resting. Tom calls the States, the Wildlife Conservation Society; two more veterinarians will fly down to help. Tissue samples are saved, and permits to transport them to laboratories are needed. Even in pieces, the iguanas require permits to leave the island.

Sandy's eyes are swollen and red. There is blood on her BIRP shirt. "Has anyone seen Macho?"

Timothy arrives. "I was on my way to work and heard it on the news," he says, hugging each of us.

My eyes sting and I clench my teeth and make fists. "I really, really need to find them, I *need* to get my hands on them, I'm not okay." My breathing is hard and I'm dizzy. "They *can't* get away with it."

I feel Sandy and Timothy looking at me.

"How about if we feed the little ones," Timothy says. I nod and we start toward the Mess.

I stop. "Do you have any idea what kind of nightmare? What it must have been like for Eldemire and Yellow? For Sara, and Digger?"

I'm searching his eyes. He shakes his head. Then he takes my hand, urging me forward. While he gets out the sacks of leaves and flowers, I wash my face and take a long drink of water.

Sandy doesn't want to go anywhere and she sets herself up in one of the empty rooms. She gets the week off from work. Tom spends the night in his office. A police car is parked at the gate.


Before sunrise Tom holds Jessica on his lap while she dies.

Monday morning Meg calls the airline and arranges to stay a couple of extra days. The news is spreading fast and people are trying to help. Permits and documents that would usually take weeks are granted in hours. At the Ritz-Carlton Hotel, employees put out a five-gallon water jug with a sign taped on and collect over three thousand dollars in coins and small bills.

Timothy brings a pot of stew and johnnycakes. People say they're not hungry, but they eat anyway. Even Tom eats a cup of stew, standing at the counter. He takes two johnnycakes and fills his coffee cup and goes back to his office.

The park stays closed while police go around taking more photos. They find what's left of Pedro. I press my hands against my head as though I need to keep it from bursting. We got these animals to trust us, to trust people.

I am with Sandy in Digger's pen. We don't talk, just sit. Meg comes out with bottles of cold water and sits with us.

They're saying dogs were involved and I can't stand the pictures in my head. I take a walk around the BIRP grounds, hoping to see Macho. My hands in fists, I keep turning to look into the trees and beyond the pen walls. I watch the parking area, the visitors' tent. *Where are you hiding?* When I come upon the yellow tape where Pedro's remains were found, I end my walk.

In my room I open *Peter Pan* to the ticking crocodile and rest my hand on the green, toothy beast as if I could channel Joe, as if together we could conjure up a ticking crocodile to haunt the murderers for the rest of their lives.

I lie down on the bed and look at the ceiling and start talking to God, something I've never done much of. I say, *Let Billy live, please. And help Sandy.* I ask, *Please, God, let Pedro be dead when that happened to him, okay?* Then I say,

*God, let me have a go at them.* But I know God doesn't make that sort of arrangement. So I draw my sword with a *shing!* Lopping off their heads would be too quick, though. I run at them and strangle and kick and make my hands like claws and tear, wanting them to hurt the way Digger and Eldemire and Pedro and the others did. But nothing happens—they melt away like wax, and I remember the black snake. I tried to end his suffering, tried to pull the shovel from Farmer Bryer. I prayed then, too: I asked God to please let him be dead.

When Tom gets back from a meeting about the autopsies, he pours a cup of coffee and goes outside. I stand at the sink and see him through the window. He goes to the square of yellow tape where Eldemire was. He just stares at it, at the stain in the sand, and I wish it would rain.

The next day Matthias dies.

Billy won't eat the flowers I pick. I find Meg in Archie and Vegas's pen, writing in her notebook. She looks up. Though it's a sad one, hers is the first smile I've seen in days.

I lean against the pen wall. "What are you working on?"

"Just making notes on Archie's recovery."

"And?"

"Well, at least he's responsive enough to move into shade when he gets too hot. But he's still out of it. It doesn't seem like he's even aware of me, whereas Vegas is definitely on alert, watching my every move."

I look at Vegas, almost completely gray-brown. She's at the edge of her burrow, and to me it seems as if she's also watching her mate, wanting to know what's going on.

"You see the difference in their eyes," Meg says. "I'm trying to make a sketch of that and it's not easy."

"No," I say. I don't want to draw or write about any of this.


News of the murders has gone viral. While Tom goes to another meeting, Josh sits in the office, posting updates on the web and answering the phone. Calls come in, offering help and donations, and Josh has to tell the story over and over and say thank you a lot.

"How's it going?" I ask.

"Pretty good, actually. It would've been nice to get this kind of attention before. How're you holding up?"

"Okay, sort of. Trying to understand why."

"Something like this happened to tortoises in the Galápagos. Fisherman retaliating for government restrictions on their catch."

"But why take it out on a *turtle?*"

"There are angry, desperate people in the world."

"It's cruel and there's no reason for it."

"It's complicated."

"I don't understand."

Josh sighs. "Maybe I don't either."

. . .

On Saturday while the sun rises we have breakfast on the Mess porch, with plates on our laps. Sandy has made eggs and bacon, and I'm having my new favorite, granola with coconut juice and banana. The air is still, and there's a moist heaviness that diffuses the light. No one says much; no one needs to. Tom is going to take Meg and Josh to the airport. Meg's hair is down, and she's wearing earrings and mascara. Josh has shaved and is dressed in jeans and regular shoes. After breakfast we stand by the truck and hug and say our goodbyes. Tom starts the engine and they load their backpacks and climb in.

"Until next summer," Josh says. He puts his arm out the window and gives me a thumbs-up. I wave back. Tom drives the truck out the gate, leaving behind a white cloud of dust.

Later I sit beside Billy, who still won't eat. I see his blood on the wall with the crime-scene evidence marker. But he's alive. His arm will heal, it is not swollen, and no fluid seeps from the wound. I can't pet him, since I'm not supposed to risk hurting his fractured ribs; I can only look at him, at his dazed eyes, staring at what, I can't know. He's listless, defeated, so *not blue.*

Slowly I put my hand on the ground near him. He doesn't move. "I'm sorry, Billy. I'm sorry I wasn't here to protect you. I'm sorry you got hurt and you were alone and scared."

He remains motionless, but his eyes seem to be focusing. I bet it's my voice—maybe he's starting to recognize me. "Billy?" I want him to look at me. I crouch on all fours so our eyes can meet. His eyes move, but they are still distant. He remembers; he must. "Why can't you tell me who did it?"

"Because he's a lizard," Sandy says. She's leaning against the wall. "Didn't mean to sneak up on you."

"How are you doing?"

She covers her eyes with her hand. I go and put my arms around her. After a minute she wipes her face. "I think I'll take a walk and look for Macho. Want to come with me?"

We take the path into the botanic park. Hummingbirds zip past and hover over hibiscus flowers. I have learned to recognize one, the Bahama woodstar. The rubythroat is here, too, the only hummingbird we have back in Pennsylvania.

"Will they remember?" I ask.

"I don't know. Animals don't process trauma the way we do."

"So you think they'll forget?"

"Not completely. But in time they'll be okay."

"Remember when you said Digger knew you loved him?"

"Yes," she says, smiling and shutting her eyes. "There was this thing he went through, where he wouldn't eat. The vet couldn't find anything. After three days I was beside myself. I held him and cried. And he knew it, he leaned into me—it was the way he peered so intensely, I swear—and he knew I was upset. The next day he ate like a champ."

• • •

On Sunday Willy comes with beans and rice. Mimi has a fever and Timothy's staying home. I'm surprised by how hungry I am. I scarf down a bowl of beans before going out for my daily try at getting Billy to eat. And this time he does—he takes a flower, eats some leaves and a bit of papaya. I want to shout, "He's eating!" but I save it, because Sandy's nearby, sitting on Digger's favorite basking rock.

In the night the wind picks up and there's rain, finally, and as I breathe in the wet air and feel the change in pressure, my ribs ache as if I've been in some kind of straitjacket. The sea smell comes in with the rain and the wind picks up. I imagine being out there snorkeling with Timothy and waves moving across the reef lifting us, rising and falling, and I see the fish and lobsters and eels taking cover around heads of coral. I dream about a tidal wave washing over the whale-shaped island. When the water retreats, all the people are gone. I wake up but close my eyes again so that maybe I can see the rest of the dream. Birds return and flowers open. The iguanas come out of their burrows and blink in the sunlight and eat sea-washed leaves and turn brilliant blue.

The fragrance of coffee fills the Mess. There's been coffee all week, lots of it, but this morning I notice how good it smells.

"Hey," Sandy says. She is buttering toast and I want

some, so I take a slice. Sandy raises her eyebrows and I shrug. After all, if a tidal wave is going to wash me off the island I might as well enjoy some butter on my toast. This makes me smile. "Share," Sandy says. "I could use a laugh."

"A dream I had. We all get washed away. But the iguanas get the island back. Not funny, I know."

"Yeah, but I like it."

The office door opens. "Morning," Tom says. "Sleep well?" He sounds cheerful, but his eyes are puffy and his shoulders sag. "We're opening for tours today."

Sandy and I look at each other. We're going to let the world back in. Maybe even the killers.

"What should I do?" I ask.

"The usual," he says. "It's what we need around here."


I'm in Billy's pen, feeding him flowers. I've brought some for Deborah, too. Lucky for her, she was in her burrow when it happened. She is taking a long time to gain back the weight she lost from being filled up with eggs. The bones around her tail base still show. I have to look away because an image of Sara being stomped comes into my head.

I hear excited voices. A tour group approaching, with Tom in the lead. He's doing the big pens, since Sandy starts crying whenever she passes Digger's. He says, "Here we have one of our lovely volunteers giving Billy his lunch."

I know that's my cue, so I turn. I catch a whiff of coconut suntan oil. It looks like a nice group, a dad with a camera, a mom, a boy with freckles, two girls with pigtails.

These people didn't do it, but still. I go back to Billy, who is acting more like his old self, eating whole bananas in three bites.

Tom says, "Billy's mate, Deborah, gave us nine eggs this year."

Then the dad says, "Can I get a shot of you with the lizard, miss?"

I grit my teeth and turn to face the camera. Keeping my hand on Billy's back I tilt my head like, *See? I'm being nice.*

The dad waits a second, maybe for me to smile, and then takes the photo. "Thank you," he says.

Tom gives me a look before turning back to the group. "Shall we move along? Sandy is waiting to show you the head-start babies."

Pain shoots through my finger and I gasp—Billy has taken the last piece of banana and what feels like a bit of my finger. Blood drips in the sand. I look: it's a deep, jagged cut. I'm initiated into the lizard bite club. I climb out of the pen and go to the Mess.

At the sink, I'm trying to put on a bandage, balancing a patch of gauze and tearing tape with my teeth, when Tom comes in. "Billy?"

"Yeah. I wasn't paying attention."

Tom takes the tape and gently wraps the gauze over the bite. He gives my hand a pat. "That group you were less than polite to made a big donation."

The nerves in my stomach fire and I look at Tom's intense blue eyes and see just how stressed out he's been.

"I'm sorry," I tell him. "I don't trust anyone right now. Some psycho killer could be walking around with a camera, smiling like that guy, taking shots of the next victims."

"That's crazy talk. We have got to get back to normal here, especially now when we need the money those groups bring in. The new security system is going to be expensive."

"I can't believe I slept through it."

"You couldn't have done anything."

"Oh yes, I'd have killed them with my bare hands." I clench my fists and wince from squeezing the bite.

"Nonsense," Tom says. "I don't want to hear any more about it. If anyone's to blame, it's me. I should've insisted on security improvements long ago."

I look out the window, at the ground where Eldemire died. Tom says, "It's not like I don't understand how you feel. I'd like to get my hands on them, too."

A chill goes up my back and we both stare out the window.

"So," he says, his voice returning to cheer-up mode. "A new volunteer arrives soon. The two of you will go out to the Salina."

"I don't know about that."

"What do you mean?"

"How can we let the lizards go out there, where the killers are? Where roads are, and dogs?"

"Oh, Clarice, please. The whole point of this facility is to get these animals reestablished in the wild, not to run a zoo."

"It's dangerous out there. They'll be hurt or killed!"

"Some, yes. That's life."

"How can you stand it?"

Tom lets out a breath. "Listen, get my bike out of the shed. Ride to the beach and take a long walk." He goes into his office.

I splash water on my face, trying to keep the bandage dry. Then I slip out the door and go to the shed.


Salty sea air gets at everything metal. I can tell that Tom takes care of the bike, but there are still patches of rust on the frame and spokes. The tires are extra thick, which is good on the gravel. It has softened to an ivory color from the rain and there are milky puddles and I ride without kicking up white dust. I haven't been on a bike since the last time I rode up Route 171, coming home from the shelter. That shiver travels through me, the one about going back to school, and I can almost taste the cold, brown-leaf air. It makes me feel so empty inside. I smell the sea and breathe in as much as my lungs will hold.

Where the road goes right, I go left and pedal through the sea grape bushes. I am the only person here, where Timothy and I were just a week ago. The day before it happened. Straddling the bike, I look out across the turquoise water and up the beach. The storm was big. Clumps of brown and ochre seaweed are strewn along the high-tide line. The sea is almost calm. Big swells rise and come ashore, one after another, each one cresting and curling into a glassy tube that rolls up the beach before collapsing.

After laying the bike down in a patch of sea lavender,

I walk to the water's edge. The sun is overhead. My shadow stands to my left and I see my shape, a two-legged animal. Human being. We do terrible, cruel things. I make fists and get sick and weepy and ask why. I have dumb fantasies of justice, but what I need to do is something real.

I walk up the beach, my shadow leading the way. A black sea urchin with short spines is washed up by the storm and I pick him up and turn him over. I see the five rays going out from the mouth like a star and I remember how Timothy explained about starfishes and sea urchins. "Echinodermata," he said. "Spiny skin."

The urchin's spines move slowly and the tube feet in between glisten, searching for something to hold on to. I step in the water up to my knees and throw him out as far as I can. Salt water seeps under my bandage and I suck in air. I know it's good for the wound and I grit my teeth and dunk my hand.

Just a little bit ahead is another urchin and near him a jellyfish. I throw the urchin back, but the jellyfish has been in the sun too long and the surface of his body is dull and about to blister. I see just the legs of a crab picked apart by other crabs. The tracks tell the story.

I keep walking and find a live baby conch small enough to fit in my palm. A major source of protein in the Caribbean. I look at the little creature in my hand and wonder if he will live to grow old. I hold him up to see his eyes, like a snail's, only the stalks are short and thick. He's given up trying to hide, and he reaches out with a single claw that he must dig in the sand with. It's brown and thin like tortoise shell. He sweeps it down, trying to get me to let him go, and I fling him out as far as I can and watch his shell spin, throwing drops of water that sparkle in the sun before splashing down.

I walk on, stopping now and then to throw animals back, and I think about how there are endless beaches and storms that wash animals ashore to die, and it's been happening for centuries. Finally it's too much and I move close to the water, away from the high-tide line of the dead and dying. I watch my feet go out in front, right, left, right, left, my heels thudding against the wet sand, the sun warming my shoulders, and I feel something else and look at the water and stop.

A huge creature is looking back at me. He stops. I'm pretty sure he must be a ray of some kind, because he looks like the eagle rays, only he's not spotted and his tail is short and thick. He's brown, the width of a coffee table. I can't see his eyes clearly, but I know he's watching me. He moves back a little when I take a step forward, but he comes in again when I keep still. His wings ripple as he hovers in the water just above his shadow. The edge of a wing touches the bottom and a puff of sand billows up. When I start walking he goes along beside me, and soon I feel better. After a while he moves away, toward deep water, and slips out of sight.

When I get back, Tom and Timothy are on the Mess porch drinking Caybrews. "Have a good walk?" Tom asks.

"Yeah. The storm was big."

I turn the bike toward the shed, but Tom says, "I'll take care of it."

"Okay." I lean it against the porch post and then ask Timothy, "How's Mimi?"

"Better. She'd love a visit. I could drive you over."

"Good idea," Tom says, and I get it that he wants me to take the whole day off.

As we're getting in the truck, I glance back and see Tom putting his feet up on a chair. I remember Sandy saying that BIRP was his baby.

"The storm washed up so many animals," I tell Timothy.

"I bet. Dad couldn't go out with the water so rough." He sees my bandage. "Cut yourself?"

"Billy—an accident. I saw a ray. Not an eagle ray."

"Big?"

"Yes."

"A stingray."

"He was . . . watching me. He swam alongside while I walked. When I stopped, he stopped. It went like that for a while. He showed up when I needed him, like I needed to be reminded about life. About how life is—it goes on, and it's worth living."

Timothy looks at me, then back at the road. "Of course it is. Don't you think?"

"Yes, but I can spend a lot of it feeling sad. Really sad. Angry and hopeless. I had this dream last night. A wave covers the island and washes the people away. But the lizards survive. Even though I'm dead and gone, it didn't feel like a bad dream. Isn't that weird?"

Timothy is quiet. Then he says, "I went into town this morning. Some kids had set up a table and a jug with a picture of a blue iguana taped on. The jug was packed with cash—not coins, but bills."

He shifts gears and takes a left, and we go up a familiar street. Ahead I see the brilliant pink bougainvillea spilling over the fence. Timothy parks the truck and we go inside.

"She's in the garden," he says. "Go say hi."

I find Mimi picking dead blossoms off the hibiscus bushes. She gives me a hug. "It's horrible and I'm sorry for all of you."

My eyes sting and awful images flood my mind. We look at each other. I say, "It's funny, I thought I'd escaped, if only for a summer." I shake my head. "It's huge, Mimi. Worldwide and huge. What difference can I possibly make?"

"You don't know the story of the forest fire and the hummingbird." She sits down on the swing and pats the seat beside her.

"It's a Japanese folktale. One day a terrible forest fire broke out, and all the animals fled their homes. But one hummingbird flew to a stream, took some water in her bill, flew back, and spit out the drops on the raging fire. Back and forth she flew, carrying drops of water in her bill to try to douse the fire. The animals watched in disbelief. They asked the hummingbird what she was doing. One tiny bird would not make a difference, they said. The hummingbird replied, 'I'm doing the best I can.'"

I shut my eyes. She says, "I told my daughter that story before she went off to veterinary school."

"Mimi, I don't want to leave."

"Terrific. What would you like to do here on Grand Cayman?"

"Take care of the iguanas."

"What about the work of the program, its mission?"

"I know. The goal is to reestablish them in the wild."

"And do you see yourself working toward that?"

"Well, I like helping with the research. Tom wants me to work with the new volunteer in the Salina." I pick at the bandage on my finger. Digger and the others might have been better off out there. "At the shelter back home I knew we had to get the animals adopted. More were always coming in. But I didn't really try. What if the new owners tortured them, or sold them to a lab for experiments? It happens, you know. I read about it in *Humane News.*"

"I'm sure," Mimi says. "Go on."

"I can't bear it, the images haunt me."

"Why do you do that?"

The question startles me. As if I could control my thoughts and dreams.

Timothy brings iced tea. Mimi says, "We're just sorting out what Clarice would like to do."

"Tom says you should pursue fieldwork."

"But what if we do all this work, and release the headstart iguanas, and none of them make it, they die horribly."

"Anything can happen," he says.

I poke the lemon wedge in my tea so it goes under the

ice. "The worst has happened. The only thing worse would be if all the iguanas died, every last one. Of course that would put an end to their suffering for all time." A bitter snort comes out of me and I look up. A tiny anole is peering down from the top of the swing and I remember how Sandy told me that their eggs hatch sometimes after a rain. "But what about after BIRP? What then?"

Mimi says, "Let's try saving one species at a time."

"I need to know what's next, though. I need to *do* something and make some kind of *career*. And I'm an average student."

Timothy shrugs. "Maybe you don't like classroom learning."

"That's what my counselor would say."

"You've had good advice from a lot of people."

"It's true."

"I've got a book you ought to read," he says, getting up and going into the house.

Mimi pats my knee and goes back to pruning dead blossoms. I drink my tea and start pushing with my feet to make the swing go. When Timothy comes back he gives me the book. *Through a Window*, by Jane Goodall.

"Joe's got one she wrote for kids. Is it true that she didn't have any training when she went to study chimps?"

"She was a secretarial-school graduate."

I look at the photo on the back. She's wearing khakis, like we do here. Notepad and pen in her pocket, binoculars around her neck, hair in a loose ponytail. Her eyes say that she is happy. "She's so lucky."

"Write to me when you've read it."

"I will," I say, holding the book close.

In ten days I'll be leaving. Something is different now in the air and the light. I bet there will be a frost back home soon. Here, the days are shorter, but they stay hot and the leaves stay green.

Sandy has taken extra shifts at the golf club to make up for her week off. Every day while I'm feeding the iguanas I try to hold on to each moment like it was my last. I watch the baby lizards rush in to eat, I watch little pink tongues lick fruit from scaly lips, and I look at the spotted toes and remember Berry. And later, when there's a lull in the tour groups, I sit with Billy. He's eating plenty and his injuries are healing. It's okay to pet him, and I do, carefully. I pet him to comfort myself, and he lets me.

Since the murders we've been giving a lot of tours. Bills and coins go in the jar and checks get written. Tom is pleased, because it affords us a part-time security guard while the new fence and alarm system are being installed.

No sign of Macho.

I sit on the ground, cross-legged, surrounded by a canvas blind. It's hot, 96 degrees Fahrenheit in the shade, and the pages of the notebook have smudges from my sweaty fingers. I listen for any movement that could be an iguana. There's a rustle and I peek through the slit in the canvas, scanning the karst outcropping for a hint of blue, and I see a land crab scuttling over dry leaves. Carl, the new volunteer, is out taking photographs and mapping iguana-friendly habitat. This is our fifth and last day here in the eastern interior. There are no data sheets to fill in, but we've seen and recorded the activities of two wild blues. Since they have no colored beads, we've made up names—PG for Purty Girl, FB for Fat Boy. I look at my notes: *PG exits retreat at 9:00 a.m., basks in patch of sunlight for 26 minutes, moves away to feed on yellow-root. FB approaches from south, very blue, and appears to mark rock by passing leg over surface. Body condition excellent—fat. Departs area after 13 minutes. PG returns at 12:05 to bask near retreat. Body condition excellent, pelvic girdle not prominent. Dorsal crest perfect, tail intact, no scars evident. Attitude—calm but alert.*

A rustle of dry leaves and I look out. Nothing. Tucking a strand of hair behind my ear, I touch the elastic band holding my ponytail. Like Jane Goodall's—I keep in my head the photo of her from the book. I fold my arms across my chest and try to make my expression like hers. We both have brown eyes.

Carl and I were supposed to continue tracking iguanas in the Salina. But Tom said, "Change of plan." He gave us a camera and binoculars and said, "You're going to lay the groundwork for the next team to trap and process."

I wish we'd leave them alone, these last wild iguanas, but I know better.

Sweat trickles down my sides. Straightening my spine, I reach up to rub my stiff neck and tilt my head back.

Hummingbirds whir around an agave in bloom. The stalk reaches ten feet in the air, ending in a big yellow puff, high above the top of the blind. Seeing the tiny birds hover, dipping their long skinny bills to drink drops of nectar, makes me think about the hummingbird and the fire.

The day before my flight, Timothy and Sandy and I go to the beach to watch the sun set. Timothy brings avocado sandwiches with tomatoes from Mimi's garden, and Sandy packs a cooler with Caybrews and ginger ales. We sit on a beach towel, on Bugs Bunny relaxing in a hammock between palm trees, and it makes me remember June, when Mom and I went shopping for a bathing suit and I saw all these beach towels with cartoon characters and superheroes. I wish I could turn back the clock and be weeks from leaving instead of hours.

We open drinks and unwrap sandwiches. "So you guys go back to school soon."

"Classes start in two weeks," Sandy says. "It's my last semester of organic chemistry, and I have to take another physics course. But the rest is great, all lab and field study."

"Any thoughts about college?" Timothy asks.

"I'm trying to see myself in a university. I'd like the dorms for sure. Maybe I'm crazy, but I love my room here. It's quiet." I think of the birds in the gumbo-limbo tree, and it makes me smile. "I mean, it's peaceful. I sketched and wrote in my journal. And I had the geckos to keep me company." I lean back on my hands and dig my fingers into the warm sand. The ocean is losing transparency as the sun gets closer. "I love that you guys are helping me figure it out." I try to say I'll miss them, but there's a fistful of sand in my throat.

Timothy says, "When I took philosophy I kept a journal. Mainly my own dialogue about existential stuff. It actually gave me some clarity about what I wanted in life."

The sun is touching the ocean, melting into a puddle of orange light, and the sand is turning pink.

"Look," Timothy says, pointing to a shell bobbing at the water's edge.

"A hermit crab," Sandy says.

Just then something flapping and splashing breaks the water. The curl of triangular wing tips lingers in my mind's eye. "An eagle ray jumping, like you said they did."

We watch for the ray to leap again, but the surface is still, except for ripples made by animals below.


I put my bag in Sandy's Jeep and go say goodbye to Billy. I kneel beside him and touch my cheek to his scaly body. My tears make Billy's flinty scent strong and like the sea, and I shut my eyes and breathe it in so I can remember. My legs are heavy, climbing out of the pen. Tom gives me a hug goodbye—a big one, like he means it—and my eyes fill again. I thought he valued my work here, but now I know it.

Timothy rides in back with his arm resting on my bag. I'm wearing my khakis, my favorite BIRP shirt, and the boots Meg gave me.

Sandy drives, as usual. Sunglasses on, wind blowing blond curls loose from a hair tie, silver lizard earrings. Dimples that will really show if she smiles. Losing Digger is there too.

"Do you think they'll catch them?"

"Every day I pray that they do."

At the airport we have to say goodbye before I go through customs. I put my arms around Sandy and we have a long hug. She promises to give Billy lots of flowers.

"Will you email me when the eggs hatch?"

"The moment the first one cracks."

Timothy hugs me and my throat closes up. "I hate goodbyes," I say, shifting the backpack on my shoulder.

"Wait," he says, digging in his pocket. He gives me a folded piece of paper. "My email."

I slip the paper in my backpack.

"Keep in touch."

Before going through the doorway I look back. They both wave and Sandy calls out, "Safe travels."

part three

I stand in line, holding my ticket and passport. There's a sign overhead that says, U.S. CUSTOMS AND IMMIGRATION. Below that, *Thank You for Visiting Grand Cayman Island. Please Come Back Soon!*

I have a window seat, like on the flight down. The scrub forest is so familiar now—thatch palm, agave, manchineel, buttonwood, gumbo-limbo. Trees and shrubs with shiny leaves adapted to the salty air. When the plane lifts off I stop looking so I don't have to watch the island go out of sight. I pull my backpack from under the seat, unzip it, and take out the book Timothy gave me. I can't relax. I fiddle with the air thingies overhead and check my seat belt. I look at my hands, spread my fingers, and study my wrists and arms, dark from the sun and with scabby places from lizards pushing on me with scaly heels. The scar on my finger has healed, mostly, but unlike the tan and lizard scabs it won't fade away. My Billy mark.

I turn the book over and look at the photo of Jane Goodall with the binoculars and notepad. I try to imagine her life in the field, working with the chimps, and my chest tightens with wanting. I open to chapter one.

In Miami at the gate for my connecting flight I find a seat and keep reading, stopping once to show my ticket and board the plane. I'm halfway through the book when we start to descend. My insides are jittery—soon I'll see Mom and Dad and Joe. The plane bounces around and the lights flicker. Out the window the trees are a dull, dark green, the leaves getting old, about to change color and die. It's the changing light that causes the green to turn orange, yellow, and red. Mr. Bloom talked about that last fall, the chlorophylls and carotenoids reacting to light. I see him holding down the frog and the needle in his hand and I clench my teeth and draw my sword—*shing!* The image dissolves as quickly as it came and my fists let go and the plane is landing.

I move with the herd of passengers toward the main terminal and the crowd of people waiting. Their faces are pale. I see checkered flannel shirts, the uniform here in Pennsylvania. Then I see Mom at the same time she sees me. Her eyes grow big and she's smiling. Dad's face is tight, like he's anxious, and then I see Joe and can't hold back the smile.

I hug Mom, then Dad, and I smell what I haven't smelled since last winter—wood smoke. Dad's been splitting logs and they've built a fire in the fireplace. Joe is rocking back and forth on his feet. I kneel and put my arms around him. "So, how are the kitties?"

He opens his hand to show me Poley.

Mom says, "Every single day he goes out to the barn to feed those cats. He does it like clockwork."

Joe nods his head up and down.

When I stand up Mom says, "Gosh, look at you, all sun-streaked and tanned." She takes my hand. "Are you okay?"

"Huh?"

"Sweetheart, we know what happened," Dad says. "Tom called this morning after they put you on the plane. He told us about it and he wasn't surprised that you hadn't, since everyone was in a state of grief."

"I should've written."

"Never mind," Mom says, "you can tell us about it when you're ready. It's a terrible tragedy." She puts her arm around me. "But you're home now, safe and sound."

"Yeah." I feel my shoulders go limp.

In the car Joe sits close beside me cupping Poley. I see the little bug nestled in the softest part of his palm half balled up, as if resting. Joe looks ahead into the back of the front seat. Things must be good in his world at this moment and he's content, like I should be. I try to imagine the way I'd feel if I knew I was going back. Right after the holidays, so I could have time with my family first. Between now and then I'd be happy every minute.

"Tom and I had a good talk," Dad says, breaking my fantasy. "He said you were an asset to the program and he hopes you'll take up field research."

"Really? Did he say where?"

Dad hesitates. "No." He sounds puzzled by the question. "That's up to you."


Mom's tomato sauce is the bittersweet smell of summer ending. I stand in the foyer, breathing it in. "Lasagna?" I ask, though I know that's what she made.

"With artichoke noodles and soy cheese," she says.

I lean against her, suddenly tired, and see the muddy shoes lined up under the bench, where the boots Meg gave me will live. Joe walks past with Poley, heading for his room, and Dad follows with my bag. I give him a quick hug and take it up the stairs and drop it by the closet in my room. The sun has just gone down behind the trees and the light is cool and pale. The window over my desk is shut and it's so quiet. No breeze rattling palm fronds. I look at the animal posters on the wall, the one of kittens climbing all over the stoic Great Dane. I see the basket full of stuffed animals by the bed and the ruffled bedskirt. This is my room and it's really nice, and my chest aches with missing my little cinderblock one.

I go to the computer on my desk and find a hundred emails. Humane Network, Wolf Action Alert, Rainforest Rescue, on and on, a thousand petitions to sign. I don't know what to do with myself. I should unpack. Instead, I get the Jane Goodall book and lie down on the bed. Mom and Dad are talking in the kitchen and their voices are soothing. I reach in the basket and pull out a beanbag frog and tuck him under my arm.

Mom wakes me, gently rubbing my back. I turn over and open my eyes. She's sitting on the edge of the bed and I look at her. "That feels really good, Mom."

She combs the hair back from my forehead with her fingers. "Dinner's ready."


In the morning after unpacking I return *Peter Pan* to the shelf in Joe's room. Pinned to the wall is the postcard I sent back in June. Of Yellow. I wonder if Joe could understand what happened to Yellow and the others. Then I remember his face, watching Rod die.

I put on my boots and go out to the barn. The feeding

station has been moved and I can't figure out why, until I see it's to be near the electrical outlet Dad installed years ago. There's one of those heat tapes that keep pipes from freezing underneath a scrap of steel where the water bowl and jug sit. Tufty comes through the crack between boards and rubs against my leg, but when I reach down to pet him he moves away and looks at me with those yellow eyes. "At least you're not hissing at me," I say. I'm about to scoop out kibble and fill bowls, but I stop. It's Joe's job now.

Back in the house, I check email. More have come in. *Help endangered penguins. Desert toad on brink of extinction. Urgent action needed.* I get up and lean against the window frame, looking at Joe's sandbox. Rod's burial mound has been replaced by a pyramid of stones.

Mom and Dad are at work, and Joe's in his last week of summer day camp. I go out to the garage and put air in the tires on my bike and head up the road to the SPCA. I go fast and the hills are no problem. I'm in better shape than I thought, maybe from trekking through the Salina.

When I walk into the shelter the smells of disinfectant and cedar-scented cat litter hit me. Dogs bark and yelp behind the double doors and a supervisor I don't know is at the counter, talking on the phone. I bend to tie my shoe and see how the floor is layers of cracked and peeling linoleum I never noticed before. Behind the doors a wooden mop handle smacks the tile floor, and I hear strange voices. New volunteers. The supervisor gets off the phone and I say who I am. He says, "They're leaving when school starts. We'll definitely need the help then."

Riding home I imagine myself working there full-time. I start to get a panicky feeling and pedal hard and don't stop until I'm turning onto our driveway. I park the bike and go inside and drink a glass of water, then another, while my heart slows down. Maybe I'm just dehydrated. I go upstairs to check email again. *Stop the slaughter of dolphins. Help end rhino poaching. Take action now!*

I hit DELETE. I delete emails, one after another, hitting the keys harder and faster, down the list. Then I stop—there's one with "gciu.edu" at the end. I click on it.

*Hey, Clarice,*

*They're hatching! The first egg just cracked. If you could've stayed another day you would have seen it for yourself. No nose poking through yet, but tomorrow, we should see those adorable little faces. I'll keep you posted.*

*And guess what? Macho is back!*

*How was your trip home? Is it cold there yet?*

*Miss you a lot.*

*Sandy*

*P.S. It's Digger's eggs that started hatching first!*

I write back, *Congratulations! I wish . . .* My hands hang in the air over the keyboard. Sandy will have Digger's babies to raise for the next two years. I don't have a clue about me. I hit DISCARD and lean back in my chair and look at the ceiling. No geckos. I think back to when I first saw Sandy with Digger, and how amazed I was by what a special thing she had with him. I see her rocking his broken body in her arms. Sitting up straight, I hit REPLY and start again.

> Dear Sandy,
>> That's the best news! I'm so thrilled for you.
>> The trip home was fine and it's great to see my family. I'm starting school soon and thinking of going back to the shelter on Saturdays. It's getting cool and the leaves are beginning to turn. It's so different here.

I stop and look at what I wrote. It sounds dumb and I'm about to hit DISCARD, but I don't. Before hitting SEND I write:

>> I wish I could be there to help celebrate. Please send baby pictures!
>> Love,
>> Clarice

On the first day of school I walk out to wait for the bus. I exhale to see if my breath makes steam. Maybe. I try again. Just a little. Chilly, not cold. I'm wearing the BIRP uniform—blue iguana T-shirt under my sweatshirt, khaki trousers, and hiking boots. And I've got my hair in a Jane Goodall ponytail.

As the bus comes to a stop, I shift my backpack and climb on board.

"Morning, Clarice," the driver says. "Have a good summer?"

"I did, thanks."

I feel eyes on me as I look for a seat. Someone says, "Hey, Clarice."

"Hey," I say back. I sit down and slide over against the window and take out the Goodall book, which I am rereading.

Later, walking out of English, I see Mr. Bloom down the hall and my back stiffens. I clench my teeth, straighten my shoulders, and get ready to walk by. I almost want him to see me in the BIRP uniform, but I'm relieved when he goes into the bio lab, and I walk past quickly to get to art class.

As soon as the bell rings for lunch hour I go to Ms. Kling's office. But it's dark and there's a sign on the door saying she'll be away for a few weeks. I hope everything's all right, that she didn't get hurt or something.

I take my lunch to the auditorium and it's dark there, too, and totally quiet. The mural Polly and I painted is gone. The wall is a mess, with nail holes and bits of masking tape. I sit down in one of the seats and take out my sandwich, but I don't feel like eating.

After a while the lights come on and I turn around to see who's there. A couple of kids I don't recognize. Freshmen, checking out the sound booth. I clear my throat. "Do either of you know where the mural went? The painting from last year's play?"

"In the library," the guy says.

I say thanks and go up to the second floor. At first I'm shocked to see that they cut the mural to half its original height so it would fit on the back wall. But actually it looks okay, and the way the trees are cut off at midtrunk emphasizes the line of ants that Polly said we needed to put in. She also said we absolutely had to put in our initials. I go up close to the big leaf that curls over where the last ant exits the foliage and enters the scene, and I find "C & P" worked into the leaf like part of its veins. I trace the *P* with my finger and see Polly on stage with glittery hair in the lavender spotlight for the twilight scene. I'll go to the movies one day and there she'll be on screen, wild and gorgeous. What's funny is, I don't envy her that. I just wish I had her courage.

There's a full moon, and a frost that seems to hurry the leaves to yellow and orange. My suntan is faded and I've put away my BIRP uniform and I'm back to jeans and sweaters.

Finally, Sandy emails.

*Hi, Clarice!*

*Sorry I took so long writing back. I've been working extra shifts so I can get time off when I need to study for finals. And things are incredibly busy here.*

*Can you believe that every single egg hatched and now we've got close to a hundred new babies! Boy, could we use your help. Since school started we don't have quite as many tour groups, but they're still coming.*

*We're having stormy weather, so there's tension in the air. No news. Somebody out there knows. But no one is talking.*

*Love,*

*Sandy*

*P.S. Check out the pics, especially the one that looks like a little Digger. I'm calling him Little Guy. Isn't he totally precious?*

I open the attachment. He's nestled in the palm of her hand, stubby nose, huge eyes, fat belly, and all stripy and speckled and scarcely a trace of blue. He's so perfect, with each little spine in his crest intact, each tiny curved claw. I download the photo and install it on my desktop and then I write back to say thanks for the pics and that I hope they catch the ones who did it soon.

Over the next few days I constantly check email, but I don't write to Sandy again, because I know she's busy. I visit the BIRP site and scroll past the story and photos of what happened and get to my favorite, the one of Meg and Josh at the edge of the Salina, and I sit there, looking at it.

I start working at the shelter, just Saturdays. I ride my bike there one cold October morning. The light is dim, and there's a layer of gray cotton clouds that's so close it feels as though it's tucking us in for winter.

After cleanup I check in with a puppy who got dropped off in a box, with a deep gash in his back. He's a brindled pit bull–Lab mix with a white bib and paws and he should have a round stomach, like all puppies so young, but he doesn't. The veterinarian made neat stitches, but he'll always have a bad scar. I look at the wound, which we know nothing about. I try to imagine how it happened, but then I stop myself. What he needs is for me to give him some kindness. "Hello, Boy," I say.

Sitting down on the floor I spread a towel in front of me and open the cage door. He pees and cries and it makes me want to cry, but I keep talking and finally he lets me slip a hand under and pull him out. He whimpers and presses against my leg as I pet him, taking care not to brush against the sutures. "What if I call you Billy?" I whisper, my throat tight. "Would that be okay?" I tell him about the other Billy while I stroke his ears and chest. Soon he is relaxed enough to lie down so I can pet his belly, which puts him to sleep.

Outside it's getting dark, and there are snow flurries. My dad pulls up and loads my bicycle in the back. Now that it's cold, riding in the truck is easier. There are deer around, but Dad isn't driving fast, so I can relax and look at the white-dusted fields lit up by the moon.

"Clarice," he says. "How's it going?"

"Okay."

"Are you missing a boy?"

"Yeah. Billy. He's a lizard." Dad's still got that anxious thing, like at the airport, and so I ask, "Are you all right?

You're not, like, sick or anything, are you? Or Mom?"

"We're fine. But we are concerned. Do you really want to live here after you graduate? Don't misunderstand—your mother and I are happy to have you home. God knows we can use the help with Joe. But is that what you want?"

"I can't talk about it now. It's too complicated."

"What's complicated? What part?"

I let out a breath that sinks my chest. "It just feels like there's nowhere for me to be. I'm not all set like everyone else—like Sandy and the others. I'm not so talented and sure, like Polly. No big scientist is going to discover me, the way Dr. Leakey found Jane Goodall."

"Clarice, each of those people got where they are by taking steps. Big ones, little ones, it doesn't matter. You just took a huge step this summer. Why not take the next?"

A car comes up behind, filling the cab with light. Dad puts on the signal and goes halfway onto the shoulder, the car passes, and all is dark again, except for moonlight reflected off snow. Neither of us speaks, and when we get to the top of the hill I see our house with lights on and smoke coming out the chimney.

Dad makes the turn into the driveway. "Come talk to us if there's something we can help with, okay?"

"Okay, Dad. Thanks for the ride." I hang my coat in the mudroom and call out, "Hi, Mom," and run upstairs to check email. *Help stop the slaughter. Take Action Now. Extinction Alert.* Delete, delete. I sit there staring at the screen until flamingoes materialize, long necks out and flapping brilliant pink, then fading into monarch butterflies. I take out my journal, which I haven't opened since before the murders. Slowly I turn the pages and look at my notes and drawings. I like them.

I find the slip of paper with Timothy's email and wake up the computer.

*Dear Timothy,*

*I love* Through a Window. *I read most of it on the plane, and I'm reading it again. I didn't know she had a baby and raised him in the bush while she was studying the chimps. And the part in the beginning, when she's watching them play, and there's a thunderstorm? It's as though she's telling a story. I try to make my drawings and notes do that. I think we're alike, just a little. I'm not saying I could ever be a great field biologist like her, I just mean we think and feel the same when it comes to animals. Especially about cruelty. The photo of the chimp with the chain around his neck made me shut the book. But finally I looked at the photos and read every word. I couldn't believe the one of the chimp in the cage who was so desperate for contact he reached through the bars to groom her hand. If I were in her shoes, I couldn't have left the lab without him. They'd have dragged me out in handcuffs.*

*When she talks about cruelty, and the environmental problems and how there are fewer and fewer chimps in the wild, she says, What differ-*

*ence could I possibly make? That's what I said to*
*Mimi, and she told me about the hummingbird*
*and the fire. Please give Mimi a big hug from me.*
   *Yours,*
   *Clarice*


Sunday afternoon I'm carving a pumpkin on the porch when an old blue Chevy turns onto our driveway. Polly gets out, dressed in black leggings and boots and about five inches of silver bracelets on her wrist. "I knew you'd be back by now," she says, hugging me tight. "I just read your post-card—I hadn't been home since June."

I take Polly's arm. "Do you have time for a walk?"

We go up the path to the field where Dad gave me driving lessons. "First," Polly says, "you gotta tell me about the beach. Was it white sand forever and turquoise-blue water?"

"Exactly like that, and I went snorkeling, too. Promise me you'll do it one day—go snorkeling, or diving. It's incredible, actually being *in* the ocean, with the fish swimming all around you. We saw a barracuda, long as I am, and these eagle rays. The way they circled, it was like they were flying under water."

"'We'?"

"Yeah. Timothy."

"Then you *did* meet a guy."

"A friend, Polly. This totally cool guy who's a marine bio major."

"Uh-huh. So what about the blue lizards?"

"You wouldn't believe them—they're *huge*, and they have red eyes." I tell her about Billy, and Berry. And about what happened.

"People are sick," she says, shaking her head.

I'm quiet a moment. Then I tell her, "I went out in the field with these biologists. I think it's what I want. If I can get there from here."

"Why wouldn't you?"

"I don't know, just—" I stop walking and let out a breath that makes steam.

Polly's shoulders go up. "It's getting cold. And it must be, what, around four? I'm taking the six o'clock bus."

We turn back and I say, "You haven't told me anything about you. What's your apartment like? Did you find a job?"

"Yep, got a job, got an apartment. Actually, I've got a room in an apartment I'm sharing with another actor. It's midtown on the West Side and the restaurant's on the Lower East Side. I just take the train downtown and walk across."

"Did you say act*or*?"

"He's not into girls."

"Still, what's that like?"

"Great. Like hanging with my brother. Even better, since we don't fight over stupid stuff. And we support each other in our acting."

"So when's your big debut?"

"I gotta learn how to act, first. I'm taking classes Tuesdays and Thursdays. Plus I'm volunteering with this theater company that gets kids acting and writing their own plays. I'm meeting lots of directors and filmmakers."

"God, you've got it all figured out."

"I don't know about that, but I am doing what makes sense to me right now."

We walk the rest of the way with our hands in our pockets.

She gives me a hug. "I'll call you the next time my roommate leaves for the weekend. You can take a bus in. I'll show you the theater where I'm working."

"That would be so cool."

Polly gets in the car, turns around, and goes out the driveway. She taps the horn and I wave.

Inside, my mom is in the window seat, reading, but I feel her looking at me over the top of her glasses, so I go to her. She closes the book and shifts her feet so I can sit, and she hands me a pillow to lean my back against. "Did you have a nice visit?"

"Uh-huh," I say, fiddling with a tassel.

"What's on your mind?"

"Everything is easy for her. I mean, it's like she's not afraid, she just goes ahead and does things."

"And you're afraid?"

I shrug.

"Clarice, what do you want?"

"I want to go back."

"Well, that's fine for summer, but what about college?"

"I know, I know. I just haven't found anything yet."

"Have you tried?"

We look at each other. I shake my head.

· · ·

On Monday during free period I go to Ms. Kling's office and the light is on, but she's with someone. I wait in the hall. Soon I hear chairs moving and heels clicking toward the door, and I get a little wave of nerves. The student leaves and Ms. Kling steps out.

"Clarice," she says, taking my hand. "I'm sorry I wasn't here when school started. My mother was ill and I needed to be with her."

"Is everything okay?"

"Yes, she's fine." We sit in the big, soft chairs and she crosses her legs. "Tell me about your summer. I want to hear everything."

"So much happened," I say, running my hands through my hair. "I met some great people." I talk about Sandy and everyone at BIRP, and about the lizards and what happened. She listens closely, her eyes opening wide as I describe the murders. My heart speeds up and I make fists. "All I have to do is imagine a boot coming down on one of them." I rub my eyes to make the pictures go away. "I don't think I can get over it."

"It's not the kind of thing you get over. What about the work you were doing, wasn't it about tending head-start iguanas?"

"They're the most amazing animals. I'd be happy just taking care of them. But Tom wanted me to get involved with the fieldwork as well. And I did."

"Fantastic! How did that go?"

I look at the ceiling and can't hold back tears, or a smile. "I loved it."

Ms. Kling puts up the Kleenex box.

"Seeing the iguanas in their habitat. They turn bluer when they're happy, you know."

"Isn't nature miraculous!"

"But if I go to college as a bio major, it's just going to be a bunch more teachers like Mr. Bloom, making me cut animals open. Then I'll go out in the field and get to see all these horrible things that are happening to them."

"That's quite a forecast," she says, shifting in her chair. "I appreciate your anxiety about the plight of animals, but I think you need to get tough here and not make excuses."

I'm about to protest, but I stop myself. "Yeah." I open my hand and look at my Billy mark. "This guy, Josh? He said you could request alternatives to dissection in those courses."

"That's right."

"And Sandy," I say, pressing the scar with my thumb. "She loves the iguanas like they're her kids. But she didn't quit after it happened. She's only got one more year at GCIU." I look up. "Do you think I could go to GCIU?"

Ms. Kling smiles. "Absolutely."


I tap on the door and peek into Joe's room. He's kneeling on the rug with all his plastic dinosaurs around him, as if they are having a convention. I sit down on the rug cross-legged. "You're taking good care of the cats, Joe."

He picks up the T. rex and moves him to the other side of the group.

"Joe," I say, touching the horns of the triceratops. "I think I'm going away again." I reach for him. "Joe?"

He gets up and comes and stands with his arms at his sides, his face open.

"Next summer. I'm going back to work with the iguanas. Like on the postcard. And then I might not come home for a while."

He says, "Kitty-kitty."

"That's right. You're in charge for good."

Joe goes to the bookshelf and without searching finds *Peter Pan* and brings it over and puts it in my lap, and then goes back to his place in the midst of his dinosaur convention. He doesn't need me to take care of him. And I see that I don't need to, either, and I'm not sure how I feel about that.

I take the book and hold it against my chest and say, "Thanks, Joe. You're one neat kid, and I love you."


When Mom gets home we carry in the groceries. She says, "How are you doing? Everything okay at school?"

"Can we talk when Dad gets home?"

"Sure, you bet." She drops the bag of lemons and they roll across the floor.

"It's okay, Mom. Everything's good."

While I'm setting the table I see headlights in the driveway. Mom goes to meet Dad at the door. He's going to kiss her, take off his coat and boots, and go to his office and play the answering machine. I looked at it already—two calls.

He comes to the kitchen. "Anything I need to know about?"

"Yes," I say.

We sit at the table and Dad pours wine into his and Mom's glasses.

"I need to go back."

They look at each other. Dad says, "Okay," and waits, his face all tense.

"I want to work at BIRP, and then go to GCIU."

"Oh, thank heavens," Mom says. She puts down her wine glass and claps her hands together.

"So you're good with that."

"Sweetie, we've been so worried. It's been hard not to interfere."

Dad says, "Do you know what you'll major in?"

"Yeah, biology. Field research, animal behavior."

"Wow," he says. His eyebrows go up and the tension leaves his face. "That's terrific. And I want you to get your license. I don't want you out in the world unable to drive a car."

"Okay."

Dad pours me a small glass of wine and then he and Mom raise their glasses. "Dr. Clarice Taylor, renowned biologist."

"I wouldn't go that far," I say. "First I have to get in."

"You will," Dad says. He gets up from the table. "I've got to return a call before dinner. But that's great news, Clarice."

When his office door shuts, Mom says, "I'm excited for you."

"But what if I don't get in?"

"There's no way you won't, with your experience at BIRP. You just focus on getting that application in order."

I take a sip of wine and remember Mimi's birthday dinner. "Hey, when I'm settled in you guys can come visit."

"I'm already looking forward to it."


I get an email from Timothy:

*Dear Clarice,*

*Glad you like the book. It's one of my favorites.*

*I'm out in a boat a lot with other biologists, studying the Atlantic manta. We're in deep water far from where you and I snorkeled. You'd be completely blown away by these rays. They're enormous! If you come back next summer I'll help you get certified and we'll dive with them.*

*The last time I was over at BIRP things were pretty good. Did Sandy tell you that Macho turned up?*

*How's it going with you? Is there snow yet? My mom is back from the States. I told her about you and she says she hopes she gets to meet you one day. Mimi sends you a big hug back.*

*Yours,*

*Timothy*

I hit REPLY and tell him I can't wait to see the mantas. And I say I'm applying to GCIU. Then I write to Sandy.

That night I fall sound asleep and don't wake up until my alarm goes off.

When a letter comes from GCIU, my stomach drops. I'm scared to be alone when I find out. I sit down at the kitchen table holding the letter and look at the clock. Mom's still at work, and so is Dad. My thudding heart makes the envelope tremble. I need to know. I tear it open.

I'm in.

On the first warm day in June I'm driving Dad's truck from town, wishing it had a radio that worked. I can hardly keep still—I get a rush every time it registers that I'm leaving for Grand Cayman in a week. I come up over a hill and see something in the road. My heart starts racing and I sit forward, straining to see. Alive. Brown, long tail—weasel— but the movement is wrong, not a mammal. Reptile—snapping turtle, big.

Two cars are close behind me, and I start braking, forcing them to slow down. I hit the hazard lights. The turtle is moving into the other lane. I look for oncoming traffic and ease the truck over at an angle and stop. I get out and wave the cars on. The turtle has pulled in her head partway, jaws open, ready to defend herself. Quickly I grasp the back of the shell with one hand and get the other under it. She's heavy—

with eggs, I bet. She scratches my arm with her back foot as I carry her off the road. Three cars come over the hill.

I get into the truck and drive on. A car comes up behind. I'm driving way too slow, so I pull onto the shoulder and turn off the engine. My heart is still beating hard.

I wipe a drop of blood off the turtle scratch and think about what happened to the iguanas. I swore that if I ever saw things like that, they'd have to cart me off in a white van. But here I am. The snapping turtle will go on to dig a nest for her eggs. I start the truck, look for traffic, and get back on the road.

# author's note

In May 2008 seven blue iguanas were brutally killed at the Blue Iguana Recovery Program facility on Grand Cayman Island. *Blue Iguana* is a work of fiction based on what happened. I made up the people, and a few of the iguanas. I've given the BIRP facility a couple of extra buildings. And though there is a university on Grand Cayman, it is not called GCIU.

Thanks to the director, Fred Burton, and to many dedicated field biologists and volunteers as well as sponsors and donors, the blue iguana now stands a good chance of survival. But the threats the lizards face in this story remain very real, and BIRP's work is ongoing. Funding and volunteers are needed.

For more than forty years I have shared my home with iguanas, including species closely related to the blue iguana. Each day I tend to my lizards, talk to them and hold them, and watch what they do. They watch me, too. And after all these years they still take my breath away.

# acknowledgments

Robert Ehrig introduced me to West Indian rock iguanas in 1992, and he has been my dear friend ever since. Around that time, he founded the International Iguana Society, which brought these lizards to the attention of many, many people and created a dialogue open to laypersons as well as scientists about their natural history, husbandry, and environmental problems. He is also responsible for acquiring Sara, one of the founding females for BIRP.

I am grateful to Dr. Susan Coates for vetting the manuscript for the portrayal of Joe's autism.

For permission to reprint the portraits of the seven blue iguanas, my thanks go out to the staff of International Reptile Conservation Foundation, including John Binns for the ones of Sara and Jessica, Samantha Shaxted for those of Eldemire, Pedro, and Matthias, Craig Pelke for the photo of Digger, and Fred Burton for his portrait of Yellow. I thank AJ Gutman for telling me about her experience with Pedro.

My love and thanks to Mark Keoppen, Diane Townsend, and Melissa Easton.

CPSIA information can be obtained at www.ICGtesting.com
Printed in the USA
BVOW03*1021070514

352760BV00002B/3/P

9 781608 981571